THE VALET

S.J. Foxx

After scandalising his family name, wealthy brat Hugo is kicked out of his parent's home in NYC, and tossed into the English countryside. There, he must live with his extended family and learn what it means to be a "gentleman," or be cut off and left without his inheritance.

Brattish, reckless, and out of control, it seems that Hugo may never learn his manners. That is, until he meets his match: a stoic, no-nonsense valet, Sebastian.

Hugo and Sebastian are swept up in a forbidden fling, and they play a game of power.

Can Sebastian get a handle on his master? Or will Hugo's foolishness leave him penniless?

A NineStar Press Publication

Published by NineStar Press
P.O. Box 91792,
Albuquerque, New Mexico, 871099 USA.
www.ninestarpress.com

The Valet

ISBN: 978-1-947904-13-2

Printed in the USA
First Edition
October, 2017

Also available in eBook

ISBN: 978-1-947904-12-5

Warning: This book contains sexually explicit content, which may only be suitable for mature readers, and depictions of attempted rape.

Dedication

For Vivi and Cal, without whom, I would not have had the confidence
to write this.

One: Mahogany & Silk

THE DAY WAS like smudged charcoal, and the sky poured with rain that hammered against a bottle green car roaring over the hills. In the back of the automobile, Hugo Bentley slumped lower in his seat, vastly unimpressed by his welcome to England. He pulled his fedora down over his face and closed his eyes against the waterlogged scenery.

Everything in this country, so he had heard, was miserable. From the stiff upper lip and cold shoulder the British were renowned for, right down to their lifeless taste in fashion.

The young man had left behind the buzz of New York City, where jazz filled the streets and pretty girls in cocktail bars wore feathers in their hair. He'd spent his nights in smoky halls with a cigar between his lips and a deck of cards in his hands. There he'd thrived amongst glitzy lights of Times Square, with wind in his hair as he hummed down the streets in the back of a Revere.

Life had been late nights and side-splitting laughter, with the occasional bottle of moonshine to pass around his circle of young educated men.

Unfortunately, Hugo's hedonistic existence had been discovered by his enraged parents but only after it had been discovered by the press. The twenty-year-old heir to a steel business had been found in bed with the wife of his father's business partner. A simple tip off to the papers had led to the devastation of the Bentley family's hard-earned good name.

Sickened by the very sight of him, his parents had sent Hugo packing. They'd shooed him to the English countryside, where he could redeem himself under the watchful gaze of his aunt and uncle, Ethel and Henry Harrington. With their help, Hugo could learn a thing or two about being a gentleman.

With the bleak green backdrop of the moors replacing the distractions of a big city, his parents had decided it was the perfect location to stop Hugo from getting himself into trouble. This was his opportunity to fix things. He either straightened up his act, or he'd be cut off. He just prayed the Harringtons weren't too awful.

Exhausted from his week-long trip, the lull of the motor and the drifting of his thoughts sent Hugo to sleep.

When he next woke, the sky had darkened into an indigo blue and the rain had subsided into a haze that made the air thick with a sticky moisture. He pushed his fedora back onto his head and turned his heavy-lidded gaze outside. The stark silhouette of Finchley Hall loomed in the distance, behind wrought-iron gates.

It was surrounded by endless green lands and a patch of woods that stretched out as far as the next village. It was a foreboding home with ivy garlands creeping up the pristine white walls. A great marble balcony overlooked the driveway with cascading steps that led to the front door, polished and black with a silver knocker in the shape of a lion's head.

Potted trees, groomed to precision, were lined up like guardsmen alongside the gravel path. Hugo groaned and turned away. These were the types of homes that the prissiest, insanely wealthy people owned. Aunt Ethel had married well. He was *certain* her husband was going to be insufferable.

The car weaved around the stunning marble fountain, the soft sigh of the falling water a sweet song that resonated in the surrounding silence. They followed the gravel path and the car began to slow, tyres crunched over the stones until they stopped outside what was to be Hugo's home for the next year.

On the flagstone threshold, a welcoming party waited to greet him.

"Welcome to Finchley Hall, sir," a plump silver-haired man with a jolly face said as he opened the car door. Behind him stood servants. There were valets, footmen, and maids alike, lined up shoulder to shoulder like an army platoon, straight-faced and pristine. Hugo could only assume this man was their butler. Their commander in chief.

"Thanks," Hugo replied flatly. Removing his hat, he ruffled up his sandy-blond curls and clambered out of the car with the help of a gloved hand, then turned his chin to observe the band of servants with interest.

Their uniforms were extravagant. The men wore white bow ties and beautifully tailored black tailcoats, with gleaming brass buttons. The valets wore forest green waistcoats, and the taller footmen wore grey. The maids were attired in simple black dresses and white aprons with ruffled edges, their hair pinned back into neat, simple buns.

The Harrington family appeared at the door then. First was Aunt Ethel, a mirror image of his mother, with copper curls all swept up into an elegant bun. She was a little thing with ivory skin and soft green eyes like his own. Her thin mouth pulled taut when she looked at her nephew.

"Hugo," she said stiffly, as if the word tasted sour. She folded her arms across her chest and wrinkled her nose.

Hugo turned to look at her and glowered. Turning the rim of his hat around in his hands, he gingerly approached the grand prison. "Ethel," he grumbled, equally unimpressed.

"Show some courtesy, boy." Ah, and there was Uncle Henry, barrelling through the door shortly after his wife—a robust man who enjoyed one too many sweets. He had a hardened, weather-beaten face like tanned leather. The trenches had been hard on him.

"You've disgraced your family and gotten yourself into a damn mess, Hugo. We've been kind enough to take you into our home and this is how you greet my wife?" he scoffed.

"Henry, not out here on the balcony," Ethel snapped. "The servants are listening. What is the matter with you?"

Hugo's fingers tightened around the rim of the hat, and he straightened his back, drawing his shoulders in against his neck. This was the man who was supposed to help him become a gentleman? Goodness.

"Apologies, Uncle, Aunt Ethel. It's been a long trip. Tiredness has gotten the better of me," he said and pinched the bridge of his nose. He felt rather like a chastised infant.

"I won't hear any excuses, Hugo. If we are to do this for you, you will show us the respect we deserve, or we'll send you straight back home and you can forget about your damn future." Uncle Henry's big hands were turning white as they tightened around the balcony frame.

"Henry," Ethel hissed.

"I understand. I meant no offence, honestly," Hugo said. It was hard to try to keep his tone even, to keep the venom out of it. What a ridiculous overreaction.

His uncle looked back at him blankly, his gaze roaming across his clothes until his face wrinkled into a frown. "Funny choice of attire, no?" he grumbled, raising a brow, trying to change the subject, no doubt. Perhaps he could feel the beady eyes of his wife burning into his temple.

Hugo tugged at the sleeve of his mustard tweed travelling coat, grateful for the new direction of conversation. "Fashion is very different in New York, Uncle."

"I'll say!" Henry said, looking down at the hat he clutched to his chest too.

From the corner of his eye, Hugo caught the flickering expression of a servant, whose forehead creased and brows knit together, puckering up his face as though he'd bitten into a lemon. He was eyeing up his mustard tweed too.

Hugo met his gaze and the slightest hint of a smile lifted the footman's mouth before he looked away.

"Hugo!"

His curly-haired cousin came bounding out of the door and hurried down the steps to greet him in the courtyard. She opened up her arms and wrapped them tightly around his shoulders, squeezing. Scrambling to try to reach, she pushed herself onto her tiptoes and planted a quick kiss on both of his cheeks.

"Dear Arabella." Hugo gave her his best smile, rather cheered by the contrast in greeting. He took her by the shoulders and leaned back to get a good look at her. The only Harrington he'd previously met, she'd visited America with her maid a couple of times in the past. "Goodness, you shot up! You were the size of a bunny when we last met."

"I'm a woman now." She preened, giving a little twirl. Her coral dress fanned out, circling around her.

"You are not a woman until you find a suitable man willing to marry you," huffed Aunt Ethel, shaking her head.

"I'm only sixteen, Mama! I don't *need* to find a husband yet."

Ethel only sighed. "Now, let us not dilly-dally outside, talking nonsense. Hugo has had a long trip. Edward will carry up your things, Hugo, and once you feel rested, we will introduce you formally to everybody else. For now, you only need to know Edward. He'll be your valet for the duration of your stay, and Thompson, he's in charge of the household staff." Ethel gestured to the jolly-faced man who had greeted him.

Hugo's gaze flickered back to that tall man with the mischievous smile, but it was the shorter man beside him who nodded his greeting.

Inside Finchley Hall, it smelled of polished wood and the greasy duck that was cooking away in the oven downstairs.

Chandeliers drenched in crystals hung from the wooden buttresses, and beneath them, a beautiful Persian rug filled the hallway floor space.

The grand staircase was carpeted in plush red, complemented by the wrought-iron banister, fashioned into curling roses that spiralled alongside the stairs.

Edward scurried up the stairs. He had a shock of blond hair, a button nose, and the mannerisms of a mouse. Edward showed him to his room without speaking a single word other than goodbye.

THE LAST THING Hugo remembered was resting on his new bed with his sketchbook lying open in his lap, and what a lovely bed it was too, with silk sheets that felt like heaven beneath him. His head melted into the pillows, and before he knew it, he was being woken by a gentle tapping on the bedroom door.

"Sir?"

Hugo lifted his head from the crumpled pillow and glared at the door in dismay. "Not now," he said, voice crackling, still heavy with sleep. He turned over onto his side and closed his eyes again. It had been far too long since he'd slept in a bed as comfortable as this—one that didn't shake and rock with the sway of the ocean. The last thing he wanted to do was move.

"Sir, dinner will be served in half an hour."

"Wonderful," Hugo said and pulled his pillow over his head, willing himself to nod off again. The valet outside his door continued on.

"May I come in, sir?"

"Oh, for goodness sake, Edward," Hugo snapped, his eyes bolting back open. He squared his shoulders and sat up, rigid. "What for?"

"Well, to help you dress, sir."

"I'm already dressed. Stop harassing me."

"For dinner?"

Hugo ignored his babbling and flopped back down on the bed.

"Sir?"

"That will be all, Edward."

"But sir—"

"That will be all!"

"Very good, sir," Edward replied, defeated, and his footsteps faded along the corridor.

At eight, the knock came again. This time, Hugo was up and ready. He plucked his sketchbook from where it had fallen onto the floor and tucked it away beneath his pillows.

"Come in!"

The door opened and his valet stepped hesitantly into the room. His eyes widened at the sight of Hugo, still dressed in his tweed jacket with tousled hair.

"What?"

"Y-you're going to dinner dressed like this?"

"I certainly am. Let's not have this discussion again, Edward. Lead the way." He gestured toward the door.

With a gulp, Edward nodded. "As you wish, sir." He led Hugo down the stairs without another word, and Hugo followed, his eyes roaming across every piece of artwork and Chippendale furnishing they passed. The house was lit with the bright yellow hue of electric bulbs, a luxury that Hugo was not accustomed to.

He ran his fingers across the smooth oak wall panelling and poked his head into every room they passed on their way to the dining hall. Each one seemed to have a colour theme. A drawing room decorated in soft lemon and pastel yellows, with white blinds and beaded lampshades. The sofa full of floral embroidered cushions and throws.

Another drawing room, powder blue with oak furniture and the smell of old books. A cluttered bookshelf stood along the far wall and a wingback armchair sat before a fireplace, which would be a very cosy spot come winter, or summer, according to the orange cat curled up in it.

Finchley Hall had so many rooms, he imagined the Harringtons weren't quite sure what to do with them all. There were more drawings rooms than he could count.

"A billiard room, complete with a bar. There is a library, sir. A study, ballroom, two dining rooms, a conservatory, and a dozen bedrooms," Edward was saying, running out of fingers to count on. "Ah, but here we are, sir."

At the end of the corridor, a set of open double doors led into the main dining room. The smell was divine—garlic and herbs and melted butter. This room was lit by candles that set soft shadows upon the walls and illuminated the Harringtons' pale faces with an eerie glow.

A beautiful varnished mahogany table filled the space, set with two silver candelabras and crystal glassware.

Upon entering the dining room, the merry chattering of his family was instantly snuffed out into an awkward silence. Blinking eyes turned his way and Aunt Ethel frowned.

"Goodness. Did you lose your luggage?" she asked, pressing her hand against her chest.

Uncle Henry wore an equally displeased smile to match his wife's, and Arabella, all wide-eyed, lifted her hand to her mouth to giggle into it.

Hugo paused in the doorway and looked down at his attire. "Uh...no?"

"But, you're still dressed in travelling clothes," Aunt Ethel grumbled.

The footman with the cocky smile from earlier pulled back his chair and gestured with a gloved hand for him to sit. His face was more composed now. A flat expression smoothed out his mouth, but his doe eyes still glinted with mischief.

Still frowning, Hugo sat down.

Aunt Ethel cleared her throat. "Is this how you dress for dinner in America?"

"We dress up for special occasions, sure. Is this one?" Hugo replied coldly.

She looked as though she had received the news of a loved one's death. Quite a ridiculous reaction to a man who had dared not to wear a dinner jacket and slacks at the Harringtons' dining table.

Uncle Henry put down his glass and sat forward in his seat. "In this country, you make an effort when having dinner with your family," he huffed. "Bear that in mind next time you think it's a good idea to dress like a tramp."

Hugo sat back in his seat like a startled rabbit. "I don't seem to be able to do anything right today. Fine. I won't wear tweed to dinner again, if it means that much to you. Goodness."

"Don't start, Hugo. Just do as you're told."

"Sure."

"And next week," he continued, "I have a friend visiting. A very good friend who has been helping me with our property business. Don't behave like you did in America, no matter how much he'll try to encourage you to."

Hugo turned his gaze onto the table, observing the china, etched with intricate gold designs around the rim, and extravagantly arranged silverware, how it was laid out with such careful detail so that everything was designed into a symmetrical pattern.

Hugo reached out and gently nudged one of several forks out of alignment, and the footman flinched visibly. Hugo pressed his lips together and tried not to smile at the reaction.

With gentle encouragement from Arabella, he cautiously retold of his trip across seas and some of the uneventful details of his days on board. He talked about the food, the classical music that tinkled away in the music hall each evening, his seasick on-board valet.

He was careful to leave out the details of the gambling he'd gotten addicted to with the rich Europeans and the amount of money he had lost in several games of poker. He'd skipped over the details of the fun he'd had with an Italian aristocrat named Antonio, thoughts alone that would make him blush like a virgin at the dinner table, until at last, Thompson saved them by announcing that dinner was served.

Silver platters were carried in gracefully by gloved hands. An array of beautiful dishes that formed a feast of tender meats and vegetables. From the mouths of American soldiers, he had heard dreadful tales of British food, but they'd only had the experience of tinned beef and stale bread in the trenches to go off. Everything here looked and smelled beautiful.

The smirking footman dipped down to offer him a dish of potato dauphinoise. Not so British after all. Looking up, Hugo caught those soft brown eyes and he smiled.

"What's your name?" Hugo asked.

"Sebastian, sir."

"Sebastian." He liked that name. "Is it good?" Hugo asked without thinking.

The question took the footman by surprise. He frowned a little and tipped his head. "Well, I wouldn't know, sir. I have never tried it myself." There was a hint of peppermint on his warm breath.

Hugo leaned closer.

"However, Mrs. Greene is a wonderful cook so I imagine it's delicious," he added as an afterthought.

"Well, if I don't like it, you're the one to blame then, eh?"

The tray began to tremble ever so slightly. "Did you want to try?" he urged, pushing the tray closer.

"Sorry. Yes. Thank you, Sebastian." Hugo grasped the spoon and piled the potatoes high onto his plate.

Sebastian watched and cocked a brow. Leaning closer to Hugo until his lips hovered by his ear, he said, "There's only one plate of this particular dish to go around, sir."

Hugo only beamed and put the spoon back. "This one has personality—I like him."

Dinner was a long affair—three courses and after-dinner drinks until Aunt Ethel was practically swaying in her chair. She and Arabella dismissed themselves to bed, leaving Hugo and Henry to retire to the library, where they consumed plenty of port and smoked cigars until they could barely see past their noses.

Henry's booming laughter ricocheted around the room until Hugo's head roared with a migraine. He rambled on about politics and current affairs in England that he felt that Hugo ought to be in the know about. Henry sat, balanced at the very end of the armchair, his black eyes glossy and unfocused.

His slurred conversation was mainly with the opposite wall, for he no longer attempted to look at Hugo, who had long ago stopped listening anyway.

At last, the man shifted his gaze from the wall, long enough to spot the clock on the mantelpiece. "Goodness!" he said so loudly that Hugo almost fell off his chair.

"Look at the time, dear boy! I'm off to bed; I will see you in the morning." And with that, Uncle Henry managed to lift himself out of the chair and stagger blindly through the smoke and out of the library, leaving Hugo alone to mull over what the next year in England might have in store for him.

He lost track of how long he was slumped in the armchair with an unlit cigar dangling from between his lips. He swayed until the sound of movement along the corridor alerted him, and he stood swiftly from his seat. He swung out his arm as he turned to face the incoming intruder and knocked the glass off the table. It toppled and smashed to dust across the floor.

With a groan, Hugo looked down at the carpet, now oozing with a blood-red stain, as a figure appeared in the doorway.

"Everything okay, sir?" Sebastian's voice floated into the room.

"Y-ye-yes, fine, just a little accident is all," Hugo responded, waving his arm frantically, the cigar wriggling up and down in his mouth. He stared at the footman through drooping lids and gave him a sloppy smile of greeting.

"Oh dear," Sebastian said, entering the room quickly.

"Shouldn't you be in bed? Surely even the Brits don't keep you up all hours of the night to wait hand and foot," he huffed clumsily.

"Not usually. However with it being your first night, Mister Thompson asked me to ensure you were settled before I retired for the evening."

"So why didn't they send little Edward?"

"Edward has a headache, sir—Mister Thompson thought it best if he got an early night. Besides, he could also use the beauty sleep." There went that lopsided smile again, tugging at the corner of his mouth, strong jaw line twitching slightly.

There was something about him that reminded Hugo of Greek mythology. Sebastian was all high cheekbones and thin lips, with a sharp nose, riddled with an imperfect bump on the bridge. He had olive skin and raven hair that he smoothed flat into a rather elegant side parting.

"Perhaps I ought to escort you to bed, sir?" Sebastian offered.

"Bushwa. I've barely had a tipple. Come smoke with me, Sebastian. You're more fun than the Harringtons." He pulled the limp cigar from between his teeth.

"Actually, sir, I really think you ought to allow me to escort you upstairs."

"Do not tell me what to do! Just...just clean up this mess instead." Hugo cried in protest and took a swopping step toward Sebastian, who stepped back in alarm. Like a drunken fool, he slumped against Sebastian's frame, and so the footman wrapped his strong arms around him and held him steady.

After a ten minute struggle trying to manoeuvre him, Sebastian managed to guide Hugo up the staircase.

He leaned onto Sebastian until he was practically being dragged upstairs. With his help, Hugo managed to wriggle out of his coat, slip out of his shoes, and flop back onto the comfort of his bed to fall into a heavy, drunken sleep.

Two: Cat & Mouse

HIS DRUNKEN MISDEMEANOURS had earned Hugo an array of cocky smirks from a passing Sebastian for the days that followed. Smiles that made Hugo a little, well, nervous, and he enjoyed them perhaps a little more than he ought to have.

Could he be blamed for revelling in the inappropriate smiles of a handsome footman? Not when everything else was so bleak. Sebastian was the only face he was ever happy to see in this godforsaken place. Even his valet was plain—a meek mouse of a man who was all pink-faced and weary-eyed.

It was Hugo's third day at Finchley Hall, and he was perched on the edge of his canopy bed, his legs folded, with a limp cigarette dangling from his mouth. In his hands, he twirled the handle of a closed pocket knife, hued with the patterns of the forest from which it was carved. His thumb ran along the smooth edges and, every so often, he flicked his wrist so the blade sprang free, only to click it smoothly back into its case.

His bare feet tapped across the old wood floor, and his gaze flickered between the tool and the pastel-yellow floral wallpaper decorating his room. He had to find *something* to do. There were only so many walks he could take, so many hunting trips he could accompany Henry on. He was bored of books, of sketches, of tinkling away at the piano...

"Have you ever had a valet before, sir?" Edward's voice made Hugo startle. His heart cartwheeled into a tizzy, and he swung around to look at him.

"Goodness, Eddy, forgot you were there," he said around the butt of his cigarette, affronted. Hugo's brows knit together and a deep crease wrinkled over his forehead. "Why'd you ask that?" He slipped the pocket knife away into his bedside drawer and then slumped back against the wooden pillar of his bed and finally pulled the cigarette from his mouth to flick off the slither of ash that clung to it.

"Well, you won't let me do anything," Edward grumbled, his cheeks burning red. He focused on the floor as he spoke. "You insist on dressing yourself, you won't let me tidy your things... you...you wouldn't even let me help you unpack." He wrinkled his nose.

"Ah, Eddy. Perhaps that's because some of the things I packed aren't for your eyes," Hugo answered, tapping at his nose.

Edward frowned.

"Oh, honestly, Edward, if you're going to hover around me like a damn shadow, you might as well go." Hugo waved his hand toward the door in a shooing gesture. "I feel like an infant with you hanging around here silently. I'll leave more things for you to do next time. Off with you now." He stabbed the head of his cigarette furiously into his ashtray.

"Sir, I—"

"Out!"

Edward huffed and turned to head for the door. "Very well, sir. I'll be back to help you dress for dinner."

"Can't wait," Hugo replied flatly, and with that, he fell back onto the bed in a heap, left alone with only the twittering birds outside of his window for company.

AFTER ANOTHER RESTLESS night of trying to sleep away the boredom, the sun finally began to colour the sky with a pale yellow glow. Soft light streamed through the paned windows and kissed his face with the promise of a new day, but Hugo did not want to move.

In fact, he wriggled further beneath the covers until only a tuft of his hair stuck out of the top. Hiding there in the confines of his duvet would only last until Uncle Henry lost his patience. Today, he was supposed to accompany him to Whitby to look at a potential property investment. The first of many things he would be dragged to, he was sure.

He had asked Edward to wake him up if he still hadn't called for him by eight. It seemed much later than eight—and then there it was, an unwelcome thud at his bedroom door.

"Ugh...come in," Hugo groaned, not ready to face sullen-faced Edward this morning, but he supposed that was all part of this torture. He was sure Henry had given him Edward on purpose. To spite him.

Apprehensive, he peeled the covers away from his face and turned to glare at the door. This morning, he would give the mouse a lecture about his shoddy timekeeping.

The door creaked open and a pleasantly familiar face appeared.

"Sebastian?" Hugo said, trying to keep the smile out of his startled tone.

"Good morning, sir. Edward fell ill in the middle of the night. Mister Thompson asked for me to step in as your valet for the time being," he explained. As he stepped around the door, he balanced a silver breakfast tray in his hands.

"How terrible," Hugo grumbled, rubbing his eyes.

"That Edward is ill or that I'm your replacement, sir?"

"Both."

Sebastian only smiled and placed the breakfast tray down onto the bedside table, the teacup wobbling unsteadily as he did.

Upon straightening back up, he paused and his brown gaze met Hugo's. "Sleep well, sir?"

"Not really."

"Suppose it's difficult to get used to a new place."

"There's a little more to it than that," Hugo replied sourly, catching a burst of scents—sweet, mellow fragrances from the bowl of sliced fruit now at his side. He reached out to take the bowl, and Sebastian pressed the spoon into his other hand.

"Makes a nice change from porridge," Hugo said, trying not to sound too enthusiastic as he bit into a slice of strawberry, enjoying the full-bodied flavour that exploded against his taste buds.

When he looked up, he found Sebastian had leaned closer.

Hugo swallowed, a little startled.

Sebastian parted his lips ever so slightly and subtly licked the bottom one so his mouth was wet with saliva. Hugo watched, a little fascinated with the mouth that was slowly lifting into that carefree, lopsided smile.

Hugo wondered what it might taste like. Cool peppermint like the scent on Sebastian's breath. Or perhaps rich and earthy like the cheap tobacco he knew Sebastian liked to smoke.

A silence fell between them, quiet and still until Hugo swore he could hear the thrumming of his heart in his chest. The sound grew in volume the longer those brown eyes stared him down.

"What in heaven's name are you staring at?" Hugo snapped at last.

"Sorry, sir. It's just...well, are you okay?"

"What?"

Sebastian stepped back and fixed Hugo with a serious look. "You look positively terrible this morning. All sickly and flushed." He leaned forward again and pressed his cold hand to Hugo's forehead.

Hugo jumped under his icy touch. "Bushwa!"

Sebastian clicked his tongue dismissively. "Sir, you're practically glowing."

Sebastian wasn't wrong. His cheeks burned furiously, and he imagined his ivory skin was now scarlet with shame, right up to his ears.

Sebastian tutted again and removed his hand.

"Yes, fine, I'm hot!" But not because he was unwell, but because Sebastian made his skin prickle with arousal.

Sebastian's face remained that wrinkled, confused expression that Hugo was quickly learning to love, and the slope of his mouth twitched with frustration. "Well, we cannot have you becoming ill too. You ought to cool down..." And without a word of warning, he grasped Hugo's bed sheets and began to pull them down until Hugo shrieked with alarm. His fingers scrambled to grasp at the material before it could be pulled any lower.

With his chest now on display, leaving him covered only from the waist down, Hugo was feeling rather vulnerable beneath Sebastian's curious attention.

"What in God's name are you doing, Sebastian?" he snarled.

"Why, sir, cooling you down."

"I am not ill. Stop mollycoddling me!"

"I didn't—"

"Just shut your mouth and get me dressed," he yelled, dropping the bowl back down onto the breakfast tray.

Affronted, Sebastian nodded obediently.

Hugo immediately felt the ache of guilt in his chest, and his shoulders slumped as he watched Sebastian turn away, perhaps embarrassed by his impulsive reaction to Hugo's red cheeks. What kind of valet tried to tear the covers off their master in the mornings? Damn Finchley Hall and all its ridiculousness.

Hugo sighed as Sebastian headed over to the wardrobe.

Sebastian tipped his head back and groaned in agony when he opened it up. "Why is there so much colour?"

Hugo snorted. "You're such a bluenose." He pulled the covers back up over his body.

"You baffle me with these Americanisms, sir." Sebastian whipped back around and held a coat hanger into the air. Hanging on the end was a plum dinner jacket. With his nose wrinkled and brows low, he frowned. "May I ask—"

"No."

"Very well." Sebastian hung the offensive garment back up onto the clothes rail, shaking his head.

Hugo rolled his eyes, pondering why he let this man get away with such insolence. But now that Sebastian's back was turned, Hugo took the opportunity to slide out of bed. He was greeted by cool air that brushed along his bare arms, which instantly puckered with goose bumps.

He wriggled his toes against the cold bedroom floor. "Just get me something with a bit of life, but not too outrageous. I don't wish to make my poor Aunt Ethel faint."

"I don't have many options..."

"Have you always been this impudent?"

"I have, sir. Although something tells me you don't mind that so much."

"Absolutely unbelievable, aren't you?" Hugo lifted his plum dressing gown from its place draped over his armchair. He shrugged the silk garment on and fastened it together with the belt.

Sebastian only chuckled and turned back to face Hugo, armed with a crisp white shirt. "I thought if we do the grey day jacket—"

"Grey?"

"And then do a green and yellow pocket square with a yellow tie?"

Hugo nodded.

Sebastian smiled.

Perhaps this footman wasn't going to be too terrible of a replacement, after all.

MONTGOMERY WAS A name that Hugo often heard on the hushed lips of tiptoeing servants. It was a name met with wide eyes and fear. It was the name of a lord from Yorkshire who visited from time to time—a good friend and business associate of Uncle Henry. He was due to make an appearance this afternoon, and the household staff were suddenly scurrying and scrambling around to get things "organised" for the occasion.

Even Sebastian got roped back into his old duties, polishing the Harringtons' finest crystal whisky glasses and decanters with the other footmen.

With Edward still feeling terribly unwell for the third day in a row, the staff were feeling the pinch, and Thompson seemed to be growing more and more concerned.

Whoever this man was, he surely had a strong effect on the household. Even Sebastian's smug smiles had completely faded. Hugo hadn't seen a single one for the entire day.

So, when the time came and the hum of the Harringtons' Rolls Royce purred down the driveway, Hugo joined the greeting party, beneath a grey-blue sky, to get a glance at the mighty Jacob Montgomery.

Montgomery lifted a large hand into the air to wave his greeting as he stepped out of the car without thanking the chauffeur and near ran up the gravel path to greet the Harringtons, their nephew, and their parade of servants who stood stiffly behind.

His roaring laughter was the first thing Hugo noticed about him, deep and guttural. The man was a lion, tall and proud with broad shoulders and a huge barrel chest. He was red in the face with small grey eyes and thin red hair he kept combed back.

First, he kissed Ethel and Arabella on the cheek, ruffling her hair much to her absolute horror. Then, he turned to Uncle Henry and slapped him fondly on the back in greeting. Once he was done, he turned his attention onto Hugo.

"Well, well! If it isn't the infamous Hugo Bentley! I've heard a lot about you."

"You have?" Hugo grunted, and his gaze wandered to Uncle Henry who was avoiding looking anywhere but in his nephew's direction.

"Not to worry, Henry, my wife's safely at home." He guffawed and slapped Hugo on the back.

Aunt Ethel made a loud sound of disapproval at that comment and turned her face away.

If Montgomery noticed, he didn't care. "Where's the whisky? I want to drink with the American!"

Hugo raised a brow, squared his shoulders, and turned his chin toward Montgomery. "Already a terrible influence on me, Lord Montgomery," he said carefully, trying to keep the irritation out of his tone. The wife comment had been uncalled for. "I'm not sure Uncle Henry would want me to drink too much."

"Come now, let's not worry about such formalities," he said, grabbing Hugo by the shoulder and hauling him toward the house. "I'm sure old Henry won't mind it today."

"I don't mind. So long as Hugo remembers himself."

"There we go. You're in the clear. Now, gents, let's talk business."

Montgomery pulled Hugo in the direction of the house and past the line of waiting servants. As he passed Sebastian, Montgomery clapped a shovel-sized hand onto his shoulder. "You, you'll be my valet again like usual, no?"

Sebastian hesitated, mouth falling open, but he said nothing, only looked to Hugo with a desperate plea in his eyes.

Hugo frowned. "Sorry, Montgomery, his hands are already full with me *and* footman duties."

Montgomery paused and turned around to look at Hugo. His orange, too-thick brows shot up in surprise. "Ah! Of course, not to worry. What about Edward?" he tried, his sun-bronzed face hardening. His thin lips flattened into an unimpressed scowl. It seemed Hugo wasn't the only one not so keen on Edward.

"He's fallen sick," Henry interjected. "I'm afraid with an extra body in the house and then sickness, we're down in numbers."

"Well, I can make do without. It's only two nights," he said and raised his open palms into the air for a moment, before he dropped them and scurried inside Finchley Hall so he could take his afternoon drink.

When Uncle Henry had warned Hugo that Montgomery liked to drink, he really had not been exaggerating. From the moment he got there, he had taken Hugo and Uncle Henry into the library and insisted Sebastian pour him glass after glass of whisky on the rocks.

The amazing thing was, no amount of whisky seemed to be able to shake the mountain of a man into any form of drunken state. His laughter got louder and his jokes cruder, but his words remained intact and full-bodied. No clumsy slurring or swaying. The direction of conversation swiftly moved from business to the subject of his time in Peru and all of the misdemeanours that he'd gotten himself involved in.

Hugo had to wonder why Henry had allowed him to meet such a man. Esteemed as his name was, he seemed to enjoy himself a little too much out of the public eye. Rather like himself. Perhaps this was some kind of initiation test.

Montgomery drank through lunch and then through dinner, whilst remaining upright and straight-faced. It was hard for Hugo not to be a little impressed by his stamina, but he didn't dare try to keep up. He took his drinking slowly, and he noticed that his own drinks appeared much lighter in colour than Montgomery's were.

When the sun fell, they inevitably ended up in the library again with Sebastian manning the drinks. After an exhausted Uncle Henry retired to bed, the conversation took a turn.

"Quite a looker, isn't she?"

"Sorry, who?" Hugo asked carefully, sitting forward in the leather wingback.

"Martha."

"Forgive me, but who is Martha?" From the corner of his eye, Hugo caught Sebastian shift uncomfortably.

"Why, my dear Hugo, how have you not noticed? Arabella's lady's maid. Blonde girl, lovely soft skin, blue eyes."

Hugo frowned. His vision had begun to cloud over into a light haze so focusing on Montgomery was becoming difficult. The glassy hue of drunkenness had really set in.

The man leaned closer until the sweet scent of his whisky-stained breath made Hugo recoil in disgust.

"I'd love to get a taste of her, if you know what I mean?"

Hugo leaned further away from Montgomery, slumping back in the armchair, and fixed him a look of shock. "Excuse me?"

"Come now," Montgomery grumbled, irritated. "I'm only having a little fun. Here, Sebastian, fix him another drink."

Sebastian hesitated from his place standing in the corner.

"Quickly!"

Sebastian looked from the decanter in his grasp and back to Hugo, his brow furrowed. "I do not think Mister Bentley needs another drink at this very moment, sir."

"Do not argue with me. I gave you a command, boy," Montgomery snarled.

Sebastian's face hardened. He straightened his back and drew up his shoulders. "I do not serve you, Lord Montgomery," he replied easily and placed the decanter back on the serving table.

The lion of a man slammed down his glass against the table. "How dare you disobey me, you insolent little cunt!"

"I would be very insolent, true, had Mister Bentley given me the command. Seeing as he's in no fit state to drink another drop of alcohol, I will serve my master by protecting his best interests, thus I am electing to ignore you."

Montgomery rose from his chair at once. He crossed the room and closed the gap between himself and Sebastian until their chests met. He grabbed Sebastian's collar and pulled him closer.

Hugo swayed in short circular motions. His heavy-lidded gaze dragged from one man to the other. Their raised voices swam in his head, and he knew he ought to do something to stop them, but his limbs weighed him down and he decided if he tried to move, the whole room would spin.

Sebastian stood his ground, nose to nose with Montgomery. Hard faced and rigid, he refused to budge. He was so close Sebastian could most likely taste his breath, stale like liquor and cigarettes.

"I will ask you one last time."

Sebastian's mouth twitched into a brash smirk. "Ask away. The answer is still no, *Jacob*."

Montgomery roared. He threw out his arm and shoved Sebastian into the wall. He kept him pinned to the surface, but Sebastian squirmed in his clutches.

"Get off me," Sebastian growled and threw out his hands. Hugo stood at once and almost toppled over but managed to steady himself by clinging at the armchair. He opened his mouth to tell them to stop but only let out a sloppy laugh. He drew in his shoulders and covered his mouth with his hand, mumbling incoherently into it. Neither of them seemed to notice him.

Montgomery clamped his heavier hand across Sebastian's chest, then lifted his other arm high into the air. He brought it down with a mighty swing and whipped it across Sebastian's cheek. The strike rang in the room, sharp, red, hot.

Hugo grunted in shock. He dropped his arm by his side, as if noticing for the first time, the severity of the situation. "Wait, no—" He frowned and stepped back, falling into the chair. "B-b-both of you, stop." He lifted a hand and pointed at them in a sloppy gesture of warning.

Sebastian hissed, obviously stunned by the slap. He flashed Montgomery a horrified look and pressed his cool fingers over the reddening handprint that stained his cheek.

Sebastian's eyes flashed with anger. He sidled away from Montgomery, who glowered, standing his ground with clenched fists, daring Sebastian to retaliate. Instead, Sebastian turned to head over to Hugo, who looked up and smiled sleepily.

"Time for bed, sir," Sebastian said quickly and took his master by the arm. "I do hope this doesn't become a typical end to your evenings here at Finchley Hall."

Three: Peppermint & Tobacco

WHEN HE OPENED his eyes, Hugo's world was a blur of colours—a painter's mixing palette. Kaleidoscopic swirls and stains hurt his eyes and turned his stomach. He squinted and rubbed at his face, groaning at the pain that throbbed at his temples. His bedroom walls felt like a spinning top.

The events of the previous night had dissolved into a swamp of vague memories. Drinking with Montgomery, seeing Uncle Henry smile at him for the first time since he came to England, laughing in the library until his sides ached and his eyes watered. Everything else was gone. All that remained was the disgusting grogginess of a hangover. With how he was living back home, he ought to have become used to them by now, even immune, but instead, each one was worse than the last. If his parents nagging at him to stop wasn't enough, his body's cries of desperation after each incident should have made him think twice. It never did.

This morning, his body was sticky with moisture. His bed sheets were damp with sweat and his hair clung, flat against his forehead. Worst of all was the fierce burn that hissed away in the pit of his stomach and slithered its way along his windpipe, where it would inevitably bubble in his chest and cause him bother for the whole day.

Hugo craned his arm above his bed and grabbed desperately at the bell chain. His movements were heavy and clumsy, like he was trying to drag his limbs through water. He hoped he wouldn't be sick, because he didn't think he could make it to the side of the mattress in time. The last time he'd felt this bad was after he'd thrown himself around a smoky jazz club on his birthday with the backup dancers from La Vie Bohème until four. What on earth had Montgomery done to him?

Successfully clutching the bell chain in his sweaty grip, he rang three times and flopped back on the pillows. Somehow, he was actually looking forward to seeing Edward back this morning. Perhaps his uneasy silence was exactly what he needed, along with lots of water and a good hearty breakfast.

After a short eternity had passed, the loud rap of knuckles sounded against the door. It had the confident, melodic rhythm that he'd learned to associate with Sebastian. Edward must still be sick.

"Come in." The sound of his own voice surprised him. It was thick as if with gravel, strained and weak, as though he'd spent the last ten years smoking two cigarettes at once, twelve times a day.

Sebastian entered the room with a breakfast tray balanced in one hand, his face a cold mask. "Morning, sir," he said stiffly.

"Morning," Hugo answered in a croak. He slumped into the crushed pillows as his valet carried the tray to its usual spot on the bedside table. Without another word, he poured the tea into the cup, added one lump of sugar, a splash of milk, and stirred vigorously.

His usual hangover cure back home was bacon and eggs and a Bloody Mary, but this was England and he would have to make do with black tea and some porridge.

"Will that be all, sir?" Sebastian asked urgently, as if it were only his loyalty to Lord Henry that kept him from quitting the room that instant with a slam of the door behind him. He refused to meet Hugo's eyes or even look him in the face. Instead he appeared to have developed a fascination with the floral prints on the wallpaper. His mouth was a tight line and his brow was creased by wrinkles that aged him ten years.

Hugo cocked his head, not quite sure how to react to Sebastian's unsavoury mood or remotely fit enough to decipher it. "I don't know. May I ask why you look so angry?" he tried, his tone soft.

The pinched look about Sebastian's features deepened and he elected to ignore the question.

Hugo huffed, lifted the teacup from the tray, and touched it to his lips. "You look like you're wondering where to hide the body when you murder me." He took a sip of tea.

"There's a river only a few meters from the house, sir."

Hugo choked on his tea, spraying droplets over the coverlet. "Sebastian," he snapped. The strain of his raised voice hurt his hoarse throat. He slammed down the cup, then took up the napkin provided with the tray and dabbed at his mouth. "That is really no way to talk to me. You should know better than that." He groaned and his head throbbed even more angrily.

Sebastian's shoulders slumped. "Your porridge is going cold, sir."

"Well, as a matter of fact, I'm not hungry." He'd pretend that it was Sebastian's manner that had put him off breakfast, rather than the agitated state of his stomach that probably couldn't keep down porridge at the moment. "Especially not with you sulking in here like a petulant child."

Sebastian cocked his head. "No?"

"No." Just then the pulse in his temples pounded harder than ever. He didn't want to argue with Sebastian. All the fight went out of him. "And I feel absolutely disgusting."

Sebastian's expression finally began to soften.

Hugo held his gaze. For the first time, he saw just how pretty Sebastian's eyes were. A soft brown, with all the warmth of a crackling fire, with flecks of gold scattered around his large pupils. They were as vivid as glowing embers and as comforting as them, too.

There was something about the way Sebastian looked at him that unnerved him, made his skin prickle with shame. Hugo turned away and occupied himself with studying the wooden floorboards. He took his final sip of tea, finishing up the cup before he placed it back down on the tray. At last, the spinning of his surroundings was beginning to fade into stillness.

"Are you planning on drinking with Lord Montgomery again this evening?" Sebastian asked at last.

Hugo's brows shot up. He snapped his head up to shoot Sebastian a glower. "So, that's what this is about?" he snarled. "Goodness, Sebastian. You act as though it's any of your concern what I do with my time." He wriggled back against the mountain of pillows and let out a short huff.

"When you put yourself in danger, you make it my concern. I care about your well-being, Mister Bentley."

"Why? You're a valet, not a nanny."

"Well, perhaps you ought to invest in the latter then."

"Shut up, Sebastian. Another insolent word from you and so help me, I will fire you," Hugo hissed. He knew full well that power lay in Uncle Henry's hands, and judging by the scowl on Sebastian's face, he knew that too.

Hugo folded his arms across his chest and sulked.

A silence fell between them then—a silence in which the monotonous ticking of the clock roared with all the dominance of thunder. The sound of it rattled in Hugo's head. He touched his fingers to his temples and found himself glaring at Sebastian's sullen face.

The man looked like a kicked puppy as he stood there with his hands clasped behind his back. His shoulders were slumped in a very unflattering way. Those small imperfections were perhaps what had held him back from ever being promoted to a real valet. *Slouching.*

Hugo couldn't quite figure out what had Sebastian so red-faced and furious. Perhaps something had happened last night that Hugo couldn't remember. Had he been rude to him? Had Montgomery been rude? Whatever it was, Hugo lacked the patience to deal with it. He was exhausted, frustrated, and in pain.

At last, he cleared his throat. He did remember one particular comment. "I suppose some of this is related to what Montgomery said about Martha. I can see you have...feelings for her."

Sebastian's gaze snapped up. His expression quite suddenly flittered into an amused one. That cocky mouth of his lifted into a lopsided smirk. "I don't have feelings for Martha."

"It made sense to assume so." Hugo sighed and then threw off the duvet and climbed out of bed. He had never known anybody quite so insolent and ridiculous as Sebastian, but he had not yet found it in him to properly discipline the man for it. Perhaps it was the way Sebastian looked at him with those warm eyes or the way his lips formed into that wickedly innocent smile whenever he said anything that tiptoed over the line. Maybe Hugo enjoyed the excitement that Sebastian brought into his boring new life. His little outbursts of insolence were so unexpected and refreshing that he secretly did not mind it at all.

Hugo's legs shook once he was upright and on two feet. The coldness of the wooden floor beneath his soles, though, was very welcome. He wriggled his toes.

"Martha isn't really my taste," Sebastian continued.

Hugo snatched up his dressing gown, and shrugged it on. "Can we stop talking about Martha and perhaps get me ready?"

"Yes, sir," Sebastian replied quickly, far too keen to move on and forget their short-lived fallout.

"And you can stop that insolent smiling."

Sebastian's mouth twitched, but he managed to catch the smile before it came.

"And no more back talk," Hugo added.

"No more back talk," Sebastian agreed, and with that, he turned and headed for the wardrobe.

Hugo's gaze followed him as Sebastian pondered over the options, flicking through the hangers with gentle noises of distaste and the odd hum of approval. After much deliberation, sliding the hangers back and forth along the hanging rack and opening various drawers, he plucked out a brown tie. The material slipped between his fingers.

The tie fell to the floor, and so he bent down to retrieve it. Hugo got a rather impressive view of his ass.

Hugo cocked his head to admire the curve of it, which stuck into the air as Sebastian reached down. His slacks tightened over the roundness of his behind, making it appeal to Hugo in ways it never had before. This was a good angle for Sebastian.

Biting his lip, Hugo stared. He tried to force down his smile, but he couldn't help himself. Heat began to tingle at his cheeks, guilt written all over his expression.

Sebastian straightened up and abruptly turned around to face Hugo.

Hugo gasped in alarm.

Sebastian froze. "Everything okay?"

Still chewing at his lip, Hugo nodded, but his attention strayed down, a quick glance at Sebastian's crotch before returning to the man's eyes. It was only a quick look—a swift glance between Sebastian's legs. Surely he wouldn't notice?

"It appears something has caught your attention," Sebastian accused.

"No," Hugo said, a little too quickly.

Sebastian only shrugged and turned his back, and then busied himself taking out clothes for the day. He laid them out along the back of Hugo's armchair. Once he was done, he looked back to Hugo, who stood awkwardly, clasping his hands together, waiting.

"Are you sure you're okay, sir? You look a little distracted this morning."

"No."

"No, you're not okay, or no, you're not distracted?"

"Listen here, Sebastian," Hugo spat, his face flushed with anger.

Hugo drew back his shoulders, pushed out his chest, and began to approach Sebastian. "I have had just about enough of your insolence for one day."

Sebastian didn't even flinch. "There's no need to be angry, sir. I saw you looking and honestly...I'm a little flattered." His tone was as sweet as honey as his eyes met Hugo's and he *smiled*. "Also, your sketch pad," he continued, "you need to find a new home for it. One that isn't as obvious as beneath your pillow or inside your sock drawer. Those sketches will get you arrested." He said the words with a light-hearted laugh.

This stopped Hugo. He floundered. He opened his mouth to say something, but only horrified croaks fell from between his lips. His chest felt like it had been skewered by a sword. His breaths were all tangled, and the room had returned to wobbling beneath his feet. Oh God. Sebastian knew. He knew everything.

"And with the way you've been looking at me lately, I can only assume you are attracted to me."

Hugo gasped.

"It's okay. I have been with men before." He took a step forward.

Hugo took a step back.

"I have to ask," Sebastian whispered, "those drawings, are they of men you know?" He stalked toward him like a predator closing in on its prey. He closed the distance between them and shoved out his hand, nudging it against Hugo's chest.

Hugo stumbled backward and his shoulders hit the cold wall. He pressed his back to the surface and tipped his head to look up at Sebastian, who loomed over him with hardened eyes. He dipped down and pressed his lips over Hugo's.

Wet, soft lips that tasted like peppermint rolled over his, and a tongue pushed against his mouth to pry his lips apart.

Hugo moaned out his delight and opened his mouth to encourage more of Sebastian's tongue to work its way inside. He closed his eyes and melted, knowing he should shove Sebastian away, but he could not will himself to do it. Those lips tasted too good to deny.

Sebastian placed his hands on Hugo's hips and pinned them to the wall, holding him firm and still. The restriction of movement only encouraged Hugo to wriggle, and Sebastian clamped his hands tighter around his waist, forcing him to stop.

The way Sebastian held him tight, demanding he remain still, sent a nervous shiver shuddering straight down Hugo's growing cock.

His heart wavered, but the sensation of their tongues dancing together calmed his nerves enough for him to forget himself, and he simply relaxed, enjoying the sensation.

When at last Sebastian broke their kiss, Hugo glared. Was that it? He looked up at him, attempting to scramble his thoughts together to think up something...anything to say, but his mind only spun in a blur of emotions. Outrage, horror, but most of all, the undeniable stir of arousal.

Hugo wanted to throw out his hands and smack Sebastian. To scream and yell and tell him how wrong this was. He planned to. In a moment, once he formed the nerve to speak again.

Before he could do any such thing, Sebastian's mouth hovered by Hugo's ear. His hot breath trickled along his neck as he whispered, "I am so sick of you behaving like a spoiled brat. Somebody needs to put you in your place." He dipped his head and captured Hugo's mouth in another rough kiss, and his hand slipped into the gap of his robe and rested at his waist.

His hands were cold as they ghosted over the warm flush of Hugo's skin. They made his flesh pucker as Sebastian traced patterns along his hip bones with his fingertips. Soft, cool hands slid further up his body. They ghosted along his hip, his stomach, across his ribs, in careful, teasing strokes, inching further along his chest until they hit his nipples.

"Se-Sebastian," Hugo groaned into his mouth.

Sebastian pulled his lips back and paused the caressing at once. He glanced at Hugo and arched his brow in question.

"We shouldn't do this... This is so wrong."

"But you're enjoying it. What's wrong about that?"

"Y-yes bu- but...well—" Hugo's face burned with humiliation and desire.

"You aren't putting up much of a fight." Sebastian hummed, pinching his nipples.

Hugo hissed at the pleasant sting.

"Nobody needs to know," Sebastian reassured him gently. "It can be our little secret. Do you want me to stop?" He removed his hands altogether.

Hugo shook his head. "I don't think..." He shivered. Did he really want this to stop? There was a rather welcome warmth stirring in the pit of his stomach and his skin was alight, crackling with a heat that made his hairs stand tall. He wanted those hands to venture further along his body, and his mind was beginning to wonder what they might feel like around his cock.

"Is that a no?"

"Yes—no. Don't...don't stop. Touch me...everywhere." He forced the words out. Panicked that the sensation would indeed stop and he would regret never getting to find out exactly how good Sebastian's hands were.

Sebastian smiled. "Very well, sir." Without warning, he groped between Hugo's legs and began to massage over the silk outline of Hugo's length with nimble fingers. "My, my, you're already hard."

"What else did you expect, you smug bastard?"

Sebastian barked in laughter. "I'm flattered!" He dropped his hand.

Hugo panicked. He'd been enjoying Sebastian's attentions. They were gentle and soothing and he had stopped and he was moving and oh God, he hoped Sebastian wasn't getting cold feet.

"Wait do—oh!"

Sebastian grabbed his robe belt and dragged him toward the bed.

Hugo stumbled along with a relieved smile until his legs hit the edge of the bed. Before he could say a thing, Sebastian shoved roughly at his shoulders, and he toppled backwards to hit the mattress, leaving him sprawled over the tousled covers with Sebastian towering above him.

"Open your legs, Hugo," Sebastian demanded.

Hugo swallowed his shock at the sudden command. With wide eyes, he stared at his valet and the heat from his cheeks spread all the way up to his ears. Vulnerable beneath those expectant brown eyes, he did nothing in response to the command, only stared hopeless and pathetic.

Sebastian sighed and crouched down at the foot of the bed. "Are we feeling a little shy now?" He hummed delicately. Sebastian tackled the knot that lay across his middle and unfastened the belt. He brushed careful hands along the smooth material of Hugo's gown, and it slipped apart to reveal his erection beneath.

Hugo followed Sebastian's gaze as it roamed along his body, taking in every unseen inch of him. From the line of his hip bones that dipped into a valley of crisp light hairs, curling at the base of his shaft, down to his testicles, which were tight and swollen.

Sebastian tipped his head, smiling in appreciation of the view. "Open your legs. I won't ask you again." His tone was sharp now and his smile gone in an instant.

But Hugo still wasn't compliant.

With a growl, Sebastian grabbed Hugo's calves and yanked his legs apart, spreading them wide. "Why so shy when you have such a pretty little asshole?"

Hugo whined, humiliated, and his legs wobbled under the intense stare, but he kept them open wide. His length twitched with arousal at having his body completely on display for Sebastian.

Sebastian's face disappeared between his legs, and Hugo screwed his eyes shut, unable to take the growing heat. A wet warmth wrapped around the tip of his erection. He tipped back his head and a moan rolled from his open mouth. Keeping his eyes closed, he revelled in the sensation of his cock being taken bit by bit into the heat of Sebastian's mouth.

Sebastian swiped his tongue along the underside of Hugo's shaft, gliding smoothly across the surface over and over again. His mouth was wet and sloppy against Hugo's dick, and Sebastian took him deeper with every smooth motion of his head.

Hugo moaned and keened; his legs bucked out as powerful sensations began to jolt through his thighs and along his aching length.

"Ooh God!" He gasped, his voice hoarse. Sebastian's mouth tightened around his cock and enveloped him with an unbearable pressure.

Sebastian grasped at his balls and rolled his thumb along the swollen mass, teasing at the sensitive flesh.

Hugo's toes curled and his heart pulsated until his breaths came out in ragged, choked gasps. Unable to stop the moaning, it poured in waves until he was a panting, exhausted mess.

Sebastian tugged at his balls and Hugo yelped with delight, his eyes opened wide and surprised at the sensation that rippled through his insides, making him practically scream from the intensity. His length twitched, and before he could warn Sebastian, a blast of semen spurted from the tip of his cock and filled Sebastian's mouth with the salty warmth of his come.

Sebastian continued to suckle at his quickly fading erection, mouth tightening around him. He sucked every drop from Hugo's shuddering cock and engulfed him until he softened. Then with a satisfying pop, Sebastian pulled Hugo's cock from his mouth and sat up, letting his dick flop freely.

Hugo lay, breathless, as Sebastian swallowed his come and then wiped across his mouth with the back of his hand. "You sound very sweet when you moan like that."

Hugo opened his mouth to say something, but no words came. Never before had a girl swallowed his seed. Never before had a girl made his entire body shudder and shake in absolute bliss with nothing other than her mouth.

"Oh my goodness," Hugo cried. Covering his face with his hands, he grinned. He was content to lie there in his post-orgasmic bliss and enjoy the happiness that tingled through his limbs. Ignoring the sounds of Sebastian scrambling about, he sighed and parted his fingers, creating a gap through which to peer at Sebastian.

"Get out, Sebastian."

"Excuse me?"

"I said get out."

"Uh? But—"

"No buts. Get out...now." Hugo grabbed his pillow and lobbed it toward him. It narrowly missed Sebastian's head and thudded against the wall behind him.

Sebastian frowned but nodded his head. "As you wish, sir." He dipped his head into a polite bow before turning on his heels and quietly leaving.

Four: The Magpie

A FAMILY MEETING had been called by Uncle Henry. It was intended to be a quick gathering whilst Montgomery was occupied by luncheon with the neighbours. Now that he was out of the house for a few hours, the frazzled servants seemed less rigid in their posture. It was an awful lot quieter too.

At around noon, Thompson had popped his head around Hugo's door to deliver the message about the meeting, whilst Hugo milled about in his bedroom, trying to wrap his head around what had happened that morning.

Hugo had not called on Sebastian to help him into his clothes. He didn't think he could tolerate another moment under the scrutiny of Sebastian's pretty eyes. He couldn't stand having those hands on his waist as he helped him into his trousers or to see that cocky smirk lift his face when Hugo complained about how long dressing him would take.

Without the man's sarcastic chirps on his clothing choices, however, Hugo thought it best to play it safe and keep his attire as simple as his extravagant wardrobe would allow. He'd settled on an earth-brown suit with a navy bow tie and red pocket square.

It took a lot longer to dress when he had no help. He brushed himself down and left quickly, to see what on earth Uncle Henry wanted.

"Goodness, Hugo. You look practically deranged," Aunt Ethel cried at the sight of her nephew when he ambled into the blue drawing room. So far, it was just her and that orange cat, curled up in Ethel's lap, its tail tucked neatly beneath it. She rubbed behind the creature's ears with a bony hand and made a soft cooing noise at it, before returning her attention to her nephew.

Hugo looked down at his own attire and back to Ethel. She was wearing some old-fashioned dress, rather Victorian in style. A rich mauve colour, satin and lace with frills around the sleeves. An ugly brooch was pinned to the lacy high collar.

Hugo eyed the dress and bit at his tongue. If she didn't look so serious, he might have laughed. The Harringtons gave him stick about his fashion choices? No wonder his poor Ma ran away to America.

"I look deranged?" he repeated, incredulous. "Dear Aunt, really…"

Her glare only intensified.

Perhaps this wasn't about his clothes. Had somebody heard him and Sebastian? Perhaps a footman or a passing lady's maid? His moans *had* been relentless and out of control. Perhaps he'd been careless, allowing himself to become completely lost in pleasure he hadn't bothered to remember there were other people in the house this morning. Or, maybe Sebastian had told? He swallowed the lump in his throat.

"Did I do something wrong?"

"No, no, Hugo," she said dismissively, waving a dainty hand. "It's just your hair." She sounded absolutely repulsed.

He tipped his head. "W-what?" Cautiously, he reached up and ran his fingers through his locks, worried that they would somehow tell a story of exactly what had happened a few hours back in very vivid detail.

Quickly, he turned around to face the wall mirror and gasped at his reflection. His hair stuck up, unkempt and wild from the rocking back and forth over the pillows. He'd failed to smooth out the chaos and comb it down into an orderly fashion because he hadn't bothered to look in the mirror.

"Oh goodness." He groaned, his cheeks on fire. "Sorry. I shooed Sebastian away without any tolerance for arguments, and he didn't get around to my hair. Clearly I didn't realise what sort of state it was in."

"I find it difficult to believe you fastened your bow tie without looking into a mirror. If this is in the name of fashion, Hugo, you are an idiot."

Hugo bit back his smile. He'd fastened a bow tie into perfect neatness whilst slumped in the back of a whizzing automobile, drunken stupid on the way to a club many times. He'd fastened them inside toilet cubicles after meeting men there for sex, crouched behind a tree in a gathering of woods, inside a dark alleyway at two in the morning. Blind bow tie fastening had become quite a skill of his.

Aunt Ethel sighed. "Well, you will be glad to know that Edward is feeling much better today, and so, from tomorrow, you will have your old valet back." Her tone was cold. "You really must let your valets do their jobs. You'll give Edward more issues than he already has." She nodded toward the empty armchair.

Hugo took the gesture and moved into the room to sit down and get this meeting over and done with. Thank God it only concerned family affairs, business plans, and nothing more.

PART OF HUGO was relieved to have Edward back. He had been feeling a nervous sort of stirring in his stomach at the thought of Sebastian being around for much longer. He wouldn't miss the unease that knotted in his chest whenever Sebastian leered at him whilst helping him into clothes. The brush of his hands, that wicked smile that made him squirm. Simple things that he would no longer have to worry about.

Edward was boring, dull, stark white and grey. All proper and straight-faced, far too polite and formal, but at least Hugo didn't need to worry about what was really going on in his head.

It had been a long day, dull and tedious now that Edward was back, trailing behind him, needy for something to do. Hugo was relieved when dinner time came around. It was the easiest excuse to be rid of Edward, since the valets didn't serve when it came time to eat.

They were just about finished with dinner. Uncle Henry was rambling on about some run-down property in Lancaster that he wanted to renovate, and Arabella nodded along politely, feigning interest.

Hugo sat back in his chair. His dessert spoon clattered onto his plate, empty but for the smudging of raspberry sauce and a dusting of crumbs. His belly was full, and the taste of berries and wines were rich on his tongue.

He could feel Sebastian's eyes on him. He stood in the corner, tall and proud, wearing his ever-present smile. They hadn't exchanged a word since that morning, but for polite service requests.

Hugo slumped lower in his chair and turned his face away, meeting the beady-eyed stare of Montgomery instead. Hugo fixed him a polite smile. "How did you like dinner?"

"Oh just fine," Montgomery grunted and wiped at his thin mouth with his napkin. He raised his hand into the air and snapped his fingers, without looking at him he called, "Sebastian, water."

Sebastian flinched but lifted the crystal water jug. He carried it over to Montgomery and topped him up, then stepped back abruptly.

"Fill it to the top, boy. Goodness."

Sebastian tightened a gloved hand around the handle but poured it again without a word, tipping the water until it was a half inch from the rim.

Satisfied, Montgomery waved him off and lifted the glass to take a sip. "Will you be joining me again for drinks this evening, Hugo?"

"I'm afraid not. I'm exhausted tonight."

"Oh come. Don't be such a spoilsport."

"Sorry, I'm really not up to it."

"Nonsense!"

Hugo rubbed at his temple and propped his elbow against the arm of his chair.

"Hugo hasn't been feeling too well today," Henry offered gently. "Leave the boy to his rest. We'll have plenty of fun without him."

Montgomery shrugged. "Sure thing." He turned away from Hugo then, and he went quite ignored until they were all finished with dinner.

Once the plates were empty and all bellies were full, the Harringtons and Montgomery stood to retire to the yellow drawing room for after-dinner drinks and unpleasant conversation. Montgomery's roaring laughter could be heard ricocheting through the corridors as he went.

Hugo made a disgusted noise.

"Do you mind if we clear, sir?" Thompson's soothing voice, low and calm, made Hugo smile softly.

"Not at all. I'll be out of your way, just give me a moment." Hugo patted down his jacket, searching for his tobacco tin. Once located, he plucked it out and flipped the lid open. He ran his thumb along the line of cigarettes before taking one out and sticking it hastily into his mouth.

With the help of Thompson, the two footmen and Sebastian lifted the plates, glasses, and cutlery from the table and began to carry them away.

Sebastian lingered behind as the others exited with their arms full. He turned to look at Hugo. For a moment, their gazes held, but Hugo spun around quickly in his seat and glanced the other way, crossing his legs. When he next looked, Sebastian was gone.

Hugo finished up his cigarette and left the dining hall. It was time he got to bed.

As he climbed the stairs, he slipped out of his jacket and loosened the tie at his collar, ready to fall into bed the moment he got into his room. He rubbed his eyes as he crossed the landing and stepped around the propped open bedroom door, but then paused.

There was a short blond man in the room. With his back to Hugo, he had the top drawer to his chest opened and was slowly rifling through the contents. Hugo watched in silence.

The man continued to search inside for a moment longer and then paused, letting out a low whistle. A metallic clinking of jewellery made Hugo frown as exactly what Edward was up to became apparent.

Edward lifted a ring from the box and held it up against the moonlight to inspect it further. Then, without any hesitation, he slipped the ring into his pocket. Once he was done, he closed the drawer and turned away to face the door. Seeing who stood behind him, Edward's face instantly washed of colour. His mouth opened and closed before he forced himself to smile uneasily at Hugo.

"Good evening, sir!"

"Good evening, Edward," Hugo replied tersely. "Should you be in my bedroom?"

"Well, not exactly, sir, but as I've been off sick for a few days, I wanted to catch up with a few of my duties. Iron your clothes, polish your boots and the like."

"I assure you, Sebastian has taken care of those duties. He certainly has not been *slacking*. So, you did not need to worry about catching up."

"Aaah." Edward laughed nervously. The noise was nothing like Hugo had ever heard from the man before. It sounded forced and mechanical.

"If you wanted to iron my clothes, why are you leaving without said clothes?"

Edward's face crumpled. He pressed his fingers together and shook his head, desperately trying to scramble together some kind of reasonable lie. "Well..."

"You had absolutely no intention of ironing a thing, Edward."

"Sir—"

"You only came into my bedroom to steal from me." Hugo's voice dripped with venom, so much that the sound of it surprised even him. He was so stunned by Edward's apparent boldness and sheer audacity that his hands had begun to tremble. His own valet, stealing before his very eyes without a care in the world. Edward Hart, a family name that had served the Harringtons for three or four generations, so he had heard. Yet, here he was daring enough to try to deny it and tarnishing his family name.

"Sir, I did no such thing!"

Hugo only laughed.

"No, no...not— If anything went missing, I can assure you it was not me."

"Whatever's the matter?" A gruff voice sounded from behind Hugo. He jumped and looked around to see the towering frame of Montgomery filling the doorway. The man's words were slurred and off-key and his grey eyes unfocused.

Now Edward looked well and truly terrified. He backed away, stepping toward the chest of drawers until his back thudded into it.

"It appears, Montgomery, that my valet has been stealing from me."

"No!" Edward yelled.

"All you'd have to do to find the proof is check his pockets," Hugo said.

"Is that so, boy?" Montgomery barked and brushed past Hugo, beelining for Edward, who now trembled and wavered in the presence of Jacob Montgomery.

Montgomery grabbed the boy by the hair and shook him like a cocktail.

The boy shrieked and feebly grasped at Montgomery's giant hands, trying to pull them from his hair with no such luck. Beside the towering giant, Edward looked like an infant—a tiny, pathetic little creature who had lost all resolve.

"Please! Stop! I'm sorry, sir!"

"Sorry, boy? Sorry for what?" roared Montgomery, still tossing him from left to right by his hair. "For stealing or for getting caught?" He threw Edward up into the wall.

Hugo bit his lip. This much violence toward any servant, thief or not, made his stomach churn. He stepped forward and raised a hand. "That's quite enough. There's no need to be quite so heavy-handed, Lord Montgomery. Please." He feared that the giant would break the boy's ribs or quite literally crush him to death in a blind rage.

Montgomery stopped at once. He didn't argue but kept the valet pinned there, watching him squirm like a fly caught in a web. "I suggest you empty your pockets, boy." He leaned closer to Edward until the two of them were nose to nose.

Edward did just that. Out fell the ring. It thudded to the floor along with a bunched-up pearl necklace, and Hugo glowered. Not only had the rat stolen from him, but he'd also been rooting through Arabella's belongings too.

Hugo crouched down to retrieve the jewellery. He lifted the gold ring, thick and heavy with an ebony stone embedded into it. "This is a family heirloom. It belonged to my great-great-grandfather!" He looked up to throw Edward a glare. In response, the young valet let out a splutter of sobbing, whimpering cries.

"Oh, for goodness sake, if you are going to be a thief, at least have a little spine," Hugo said, straightening up. "I suppose we ought to take you downstairs to Thompson and have you dismissed immediately."

With that, Montgomery pulled the whimpering little valet away from the wall and escorted him out of the room and downstairs, so he could pack up his belongings.

NIGHT HAD FALLEN like a curse on Finchley Hall. The great house was smothered by silence but for a whistling of the breeze outside his window. Everything had been still for hours, and yet Hugo lay awake in bed, alone with his thoughts from the day.

He turned his face into the warmth of his pillows, breathing in the sweet, musky smell of Sebastian. Against his face, the scent stirred something in the pool of his stomach. He groaned. How could a valet have so much power over him? Hugo knew he ought to be furious with Sebastian, but thinking of what he had done and how good his mouth had felt, enveloped around his shuddering cock, made different thoughts cross his mind.

He wondered how good that tongue would feel pressed between his cheeks, wet and hot against the sensitive skin. He could see it clearly; the way Sebastian would smirk as his long fingers teased his hole. How that rumbling purr in his throat would sound when he pressed his fingers deep inside his ass and fondled him. Teased him. Made him moan and pant and squirm.

Hugo covered his heated face with a hand and groaned into it. Curse this man and all that he had done to him.

There he lay frustrated, with a rapidly growing cock and a burning in his belly. With a deep shame, he surrendered to the overwhelming sensations and his hand fell to fumble between his legs.

Five: Birdsong

AT LAST, THE birds sang their morning song, chirping fleetingly from their perches, their tune a sweet sound. They warbled their promise of a new day ahead, rousing Hugo from his haphazard sleep.

The tiniest trickle of sun had begun to colour the horizon like a candle flame in the darkness; the soft, pale light did not quite reach the rooftops Finchley Hall.

Here, in summer, the sun rose around 5 a.m., which meant wake-up time was nowhere near.

Unable to bear the thought of tossing beneath the covers for several more hours, Hugo threw them off and dragged himself upright, where he crushed the pillows with his back. His stomach roared with hunger, a hollow, empty pit.

He stretched his arms up above his head and groaned as he wriggled his fingers. His gaze fell on the bell pull, and for just a moment, he considered tugging the rope and summoning for breakfast, but he knew that even the likes of Thompson would still be bundled up in bed. Not a creature stirred.

However, this longing for breakfast was not going to go ignored, and so Hugo grabbed his dressing gown, slipped it on around his naked frame and tiptoed out through the door.

It was a long way downstairs when walking on the balls of his feet, trying to avoid every creak and groan of the floorboards. He wasn't sure what the rules were, but he was certain that sneaking downstairs into the kitchens was entirely off limits. It was, after all, the servants' sacred space. He supposed what they didn't know couldn't harm them.

A piece of baguette and a slice of beef or ham was all he wanted. Or a simple apple, perhaps some crackers, or some of those leftover sausages with the stilton cheese.

With a deep breath, he pulled open the separating doors and poked his head around, into the servants' quarters. No sign of life within. Good.

With a smug smile, he slipped through the double doors. After making his way across the floor, he found the kitchen empty and practically glowed with relief.

Hugo took his time to root through the cupboards and managed to pull himself together an early morning snack. Yesterday's leftover bread, a thick piece of Edam cheese, and a handful of cherry tomatoes. He turned around with his plate and almost shrieked in terror at the sight of an unexpected figure that loitered in the doorway, watching in silence as Hugo shoved slices of cheese into his mouth.

Sebastian raised a brow but seemed far too exhausted to give a reaction with his usual amount of sass.

Hugo stepped back until he hit the kitchen wall. His heart flapped around his chest like a wild bird.

"Sir?"

Hugo only glared.

Sebastian stood with a bewildered expression on his face. His bedhead was feral and it was hard to take him seriously, especially with the addition of his patchwork dressing gown and matching slippers.

"Sir, what are you doing down here?" he said at last when Hugo didn't respond.

For a moment, Hugo didn't know what to do. Being caught red-handed with stale bread stuffed between his teeth and a plateful of leftovers would make him the subject of gossip for weeks downstairs. If the cook got wind of this, so would Aunt Ethel. The last thing he wanted was a lecture about how terribly bad mannered it was to steal from the kitchens.

Panicking, Hugo tore the bread from its place dangling from his teeth and swallowed the chunk. Boldly, he stepped toward Sebastian. Crinkling his face, he drew in a breath and stuck out his chest.

"I could ask you the very same," he huffed accusingly. "You aren't supposed to be poking about the house after dark, Sebastian Finch."

Sebastian's mouth fell open. He frowned at Hugo. "You'd have a valid point if we were upstairs, but pardon me, sir, I came in to fetch a cup of water." He gave a lazy roll of his shoulders, stepped around Hugo, and reached up to the cupboard to retrieve said cup. "Besides, you're not the only one who can't sleep." He twisted on the tap.

Hugo watched him carefully. Sebastian was acting as though nothing unusual had happened yesterday, so very casual and carefree.

Sebastian turned around, touched the rim of the cup to his lips and smiled. "I won't tell if you don't," he said offhandedly, so casually that it made Hugo double take. He wasn't so sure that Sebastian was referring to his midnight snacking anymore.

Gritting his teeth, Hugo nodded. "I do not think it would be wise for your future if you did."

Sebastian nodded back. "I agree."

"Good," Hugo said curtly, and that was the end of it.

With a glance at the clock, Hugo sighed in disgust. Five fifteen. "I imagine it will be a long while before it's deemed acceptable to call for my vale—ah." Hugo tipped his head, distracted by Sebastian's gaze.

The man smiled when he was caught staring. His warm gaze flashed along his figure, drinking in the sight of him in his dressing gown until Hugo squirmed. The stark realisation that Edward was no longer in service hit like a blow to the chest.

That meant that Sebastian would be filling in. It meant more of those awkward stares and predatory grimaces. It would be uncomfortable heat starting in his stomach and spreading through his insides until his skin prickled.

It would mean having to endure Sebastian helping him into his clothes, where his hands would linger for a touch too long on his buttons.

It would be him standing too close, so he could feel the heat radiate from his chest and smell that familiar tobacco-entwined peppermint breath. He wouldn't be able to stand it.

"Shit."

"If you don't plan on going back to bed, I can make you a breakfast tray and bring it up? Then you don't need to eat leftover dinner and stale bread." Sebastian offered. "Mr. Thompson informed me last night that I would be playing valet again with Edward being...gone and all," he said, as though he hadn't heard the frustrations from Hugo.

"Good idea..." Hugo gingerly put his plate of leftovers on the countertop and rubbed at his hair. "But no funny business."

"No funny business."

"And Sebastian..." he started, pinching the bridge of his nose. "Once you are dressed and I am fed, I'd like you to come on a walk with me." It'd be safer to talk where the walls didn't have ears.

BY THE TIME Sebastian appeared, Hugo had dressed into a brown waistcoat, white shirt, brown slacks, and maroon bow tie. He'd leave the jacket behind. For something as casual as a walk, he did not care for formalities.

He'd had a few minutes to work on his newest sketch. Hugo sat at the edge of the bed, facing the window with his legs folded and the sketch pad resting in his lap, his teeth grazed along his bottom lip.

His latest work was a tame one—the view of the rolling hills surrounding Finchley Hall. Green moors that disappeared over the horizon for miles.

He worked with a steady hand, carefully tracing the contours of the valleys until Sebastian brought up the tray. He'd prepared porridge with sliced apples and blueberries, and a pot of tea on the side. He left Hugo to eat in peace and at 6:30 a.m., they met in the hallway as agreed.

In shiny wellies, Hugo stepped outside with Sebastian. By now, the sky was a glorious blue and the sun hung like a pearl against the cloudless canvas.

"One thing I must admit to enjoying about England is your countryside," Hugo said, sticking his hands into his pockets. He walked by Sebastian's side along the footpath. Surrounding them were moors that flowed as endlessly as the oceans, pastures in shades of lime, pear, and clover. The fields were a giant's patchwork quilt.

The soft whispers of a stream called to them nearby, following them along their path, which wound down to the gathering of crooked elm trees.

"There are so many things here to see and experience," Sebastian replied coolly. "You should really try to get out of Finchley Hall and explore." He held his hand above his head, squinting into the distance. "It must be hard for you, though, sir, going from the Big Apple to Cumberland."

Hugo nodded. "It's really not like home, that's for sure. Everybody here is so reserved." Well, except for Montgomery...

They walked, making pleasant conversation, into the thick foliage of the woods. The plan was to head into the village a couple of miles down, where they could pick up a pastry and slowly head back. It was nice to simply be outside and talk without formalities. It was even nicer to share it with somebody who didn't dwell on conversations about women, politics, or damn pocket squares.

Hugo was content to walk with Sebastian and forget himself a little, outside of the foreboding walls of Finchley Hall. No doubt, quiet moments like this would be rare. He'd have to make the most of it.

Sebastian swerved to the left and sidestepped into Hugo's path. He stopped abruptly and turned to face him.

Hugo cursed. "Damn, Sebastian. What is it?"

Sebastian's eyes were alight with their usual playfulness. He stepped forward and nudged Hugo roughly until his back hit a tree.

Gasping, Hugo looked up to Sebastian. His valet closed in on him and grabbed him by the wrists. He pulled his arms up above his head and pinned them to the tree.

Those intense brown eyes bore into his, stunning Hugo into complete stillness with a single glance.

"You didn't think I was going to let you get away with not talking about what happened yesterday, did you?"

Hugo glared, his cheeks flushed. "I don't want to talk about what happened."

"Perhaps not, but that doesn't mean you don't want it again," he said smugly.

Hugo closed his eyes. His thoughts jumbled, desperately attempting to think of something authoritative to say to get Sebastian to back off. However, the only sound that left his mouth were groans of arousal.

Then, there came the warmth of Sebastian's tongue. It slowly dragged along the hollow of Hugo's throat, leaving a wet trail of saliva in its path. He scraped his teeth along the base of his neck and bit hard, pinching the soft flesh between his teeth.

It stung for a moment but sent a jolt of pleasure straight to his cock, and Hugo squeaked.

"See, sir," Sebastian began.

Hugo opened his eyes to meet Sebastian's hard gaze.

"This is exactly why you invited me out on this walk," Sebastian continued. "You knew we'd be alone and undisturbed. You were hoping that I'd corner you, pin you up against a tree, and make you moan the way I did just yesterday morning. Isn't that right?"

"No," Hugo managed from between gritted teeth.

"No?" Sebastian repeated, cocking his head. Instantly, his hands fell from their place gripping Hugo's wrists and his arms fell back by his side.

Sebastian took a step away, widening the distance between them dramatically. "Sorry to have bothered you, then."

Hugo swallowed. He brushed himself off and took a step forward. His legs wobbled unsteadily beneath him. "Why did you stop?"

Sebastian frowned. "Because you're lying to me," he said matter-of-factly. "I don't like it when you lie and pretend that you don't enjoy playing around with men. You're acting as if you didn't love having your cock sucked yesterday."

Hugo widened his eyes and his heart shrivelled in disappointment. He was right. Deep down, Hugo knew he only craved more and more of Sebastian's touch. To enjoy the sensation of his tongue sliding along his cock until it swelled with desire. To see his head bob up and down along his shaft and pull moan after moan out of his parted lips.

Hugo whimpered. The very thought of it had stirred a warmth within him. He stood, with his back canted against that tree, drowning in the silence.

Sebastian waited with a raised brow as Hugo tried to piece together something to say to please the man back into giving him the attention he craved. Nothing came.

"You either admit to me, explicitly, what you want, or we go back home and I don't even smile at you inappropriately again."

Hugo squirmed. "I'm sorry."

Sebastian sighed. "Sorry? That's a start, but that isn't what I asked to hear, is it?"

Hugo shook his head. "I—"

"Tell me what you want, Hugo."

Hugo closed his eyes and nodded obediently. His cock had bloomed into an erection, and his trousers had grown tight around the bulge between his legs. His hand twitched—the aching of his dick was becoming intolerable, and he longed for the sensation of his fingers working across it.

His mind flickered back to last night, alone in his bedroom, when his hand had wandered to play with himself. "Yesterday, when I was alone...I-I masturbated thinking about you."

"Oh?" Sebastian hummed, smugness ringing clear in his voice. "Tell me more."

"You're right," Hugo spluttered, his lids bouncing apart. "I did like it yesterday when you sucked my cock. I loved it when you played w-with my balls and..."

"And?"

Hugo covered his mouth with his hands. "Please." The words were muffled. "I don't know what to say—only that I really, really want you to touch me again."

"When?"

"R-right now..." he said desperately.

Sebastian grabbed a fistful of his shirt and dragged Hugo forward. He dipped down until their noses almost touched and bit at Hugo's bottom lip. He plucked at the pink flesh with his teeth before kissing him quickly. "Very good."

Hugo sighed in relief.

"Now, on your knees." Sebastian let go of his shirt.

Hugo didn't argue. He knelt on the dirt path and tipped his head back to look up at Sebastian.

"It was a little cruel of you to kick me out yesterday without as much as touching me, don't you think?" He hummed, taking a clump of Hugo's hair. He pulled gently at the locks and tipped Hugo's head further back.

"I want to repay you," Hugo yelped before Sebastian could find a good excuse not to bother with him anymore. Feeling a sudden stroke of boldness, he reached out and popped open the button to Sebastian's trousers. Keeping his gaze locked with Seb's, he slipped his hand into the front of Sebastian's trousers and wrapped his fingers around the thick girth of his cock.

"Oh wow," Hugo whispered, amazed by the sheer feel of it, filling his clenched hand. Hugo worked it out of his underwear and pushed down the material of his trousers until his cock was free.

Still gripping the base of his shaft, Hugo leaned forward and enthusiastically lapped his tongue along the underside of Sebastian's dick. It shivered responsively to the sloppy touch of Hugo's tongue.

Sebastian purred in approval and gripped tighter in Hugo's hair. He pulled at the strands and yanked Hugo closer, until he had to hold onto Sebastian's thighs to steady himself.

Hugo continued to lick along Sebastian's cock in long, teasing stripes, then added his hand to pump along the length of him.

Hugo wanted to impress him, to show off and prove that he had something to offer. It wasn't the first time he'd had his mouth around another man's cock, so he had a vague idea of what to do. He wrapped his lips around the head and slipped him fully into his mouth in one quick motion.

Sebastian gurgled out a moan and bucked his hips forward toward Hugo's face.

It made him pull away and take a sharp breath, before his mouth covered it again. He built up a steady motion, bobbing his head up and down, letting Sebastian slip in and out of his mouth. He sucked his cock eagerly, until Hugo felt Sebastian begin to waver.

Sebastian looked divine in that moment, here at the mercy of Hugo's mouth, with his brow creased and his legs wobbling. Hugo felt drunk on it. The look of him sent Hugo into a quick-paced, sloppy rhythm.

At last, Sebastian shook his head and pulled his hips backward until his erection fell from Hugo's mouth. "Fuck. If you don't stop, I'm going to come already."

"Is that bad?" Hugo asked with pride as he wiped his mouth.

"It is...because I want to fuck you."

Hugo's cock responded with a sudden twinge.

"Get onto all fours." Sebastian's voice was low and ragged.

Hugo obeyed. He stretched out his arms and dug his palms into the dirt. Lowering his chest to the ground, he curled out his ass so it stuck into the air. The motion made Sebastian groan low and deep.

"You're such a cheeky little fuck, aren't you?" Sebastian hummed and knelt behind him.

Hugo smirked and looked ahead towards the tree he had crouched down like an animal before.

Sebastian's seized the waistband of Hugo's trousers and yanked them down with his underwear, until the milky flesh of his ass was on display. Suddenly, Sebastian bit at his cheek. The motion made Hugo quiver, the sharp sting of teeth went straight to his already-rigid cock.

"Today I'm going to play with your cute little ass. I've been missing out." Sebastian laughed, giving his stinging cheek a gentle slap.

Hugo wriggled his hips, showing his approval.

"But this won't do. Legs apart, Hugo."

Hugo lifted a knee and placed it further away from the other, spreading his legs wider.

Sebastian peeled his trousers further down his legs, and the cool whisper of breeze slipped across his exposed dangling balls, making him shiver visibly.

"Much better," Sebastian whispered, his warm breath blowing out across the gap between Hugo's cheeks. Without warning, Sebastian darted his tongue into the crack of Hugo's ass. He gripped Hugo's cheeks and splayed them open, spreading him wide apart.

Hugo squeaked and his eyes bulged in shock. "You can't," he cried, wriggling his ass from side to side. The alien sensation across very intimate areas was something he had never experienced before. "This is too dirty."

Sebastian replied by pressing his tongue into the small opening of his asshole, and Hugo's mouth fell apart to release a wave of hysterical moans.

Holy fuck, that felt good. He scrunched up his face and stilled his wriggling, all complaints well and truly gone. He closed his eyes, shutting out the forest, and focused on that warm sensation circling around the ring of muscles.

"Fuck, fuck," he whispered, as Sebastian dragged his tongue around and around his hole. Just when Hugo didn't think it could get any better, Sebastian thrust his tongue deep inside him.

Hugo bucked his hips forward in shock, and Sebastian gripped tighter at his cheeks and pulled Hugo back against his mouth.

"Oh good God," Hugo said, digging his fingers into the dirt beneath him.

Sebastian resumed what he was doing, thrusting his tongue in and out of Hugo's asshole, fucking him with it, until Hugo tipped back his head and began to let out a flurry of strangled moans.

His legs trembled and his arms bowed, losing all strength and ability to support himself whilst Sebastian violated his ass.

Sebastian stopped. That warm sensation disappeared as he released Hugo's ass cheeks.

Horrified, Hugo turned to stare back at Sebastian who had leaned onto the balls of his feet. He looked as amused as Hugo had expected him to.

"Why did you stop?"

"Like I said, I want to fuck you. I can't do that if you come whilst my tongue is in your ass."

Hugo mewled and moved to get up.

"Ah-ah. Stay put. I like you on your hands and knees."

"But—"

"I'm not done with you yet."

Hugo resumed his position on the ground. His toes curled with anticipation, waiting for Sebastian's next move with a giddy new flutter of his heart. He pressed his fingers deeper into the dirt and braced himself for more.

Sebastian dropped his hand onto Hugo's ass for a moment, then almost instantly removed it. Instead, he reached around the front of Hugo and held two fingers to his mouth.

Hugo stared at them with narrowed eyes before realising what Sebastian wanted and then opened his mouth. Sebastian pressed the fingers into it. Hugo sucked at them, letting Sebastian rub the digits along his tongue and coat them with saliva. He pulled them out, and in a moment, one finger was being pressed slowly into his ass.

Hugo clenched his fists, expecting pain, but none came. Only an oddly pleasant sensation of the appendage gliding smoothly inside him, stretching his tight ring open.

"You take me so easily, darling. I suspect you've done this before."

"Once, but I was drunk stupid and it hurt." Hugo was usually the one doing the fucking.

Sebastian huffed. "Only hurts if you rush it."

Slowly, Hugo began to relax, and Sebastian added a second finger. He pressed them deep into him and splayed them apart to open Hugo up with steady, circular motions. At last, those fingers began to thrust into Hugo, deep and fast until Sebastian had him panting with anticipation.

The sweet, overwhelming sensation lasted short of a few seconds before Sebastian pulled his fingers out. He left Hugo feeling hollow and disappointed. With his balls aching for more, he didn't think he could stand it.

He was about to protest when he felt something hard and solid press up against his crack. He opened his mouth to gasp.

The tip of Sebastian's erection pressed at his entrance, and he slowly began to inch it into him, slick and wet.

Hugo hissed at the intense sensation that forced his ass apart. He gritted his teeth and curled his fingers around a fistful of leaves and twigs, bracing himself at the initial sting. Hugo whimpered, about to pull away, when suddenly, the pain was gone. All that left was the overwhelming sensation of Sebastian's massive erection filling him fully.

Hugo relaxed. Sebastian stilled, allowing him time to adjust to the sheer size of his cock. He waited until the tight ring of Hugo's muscles relaxed before he began to push forward again, deeper into him.

"Hnnn, Sebastian," Hugo purred, tipping back his head.

"Hugo," Sebastian growled in response. His mouth at Hugo's throat, he bit hard and rolled his hips forward, thrusting into him.

Hugo's breath dipped, and Sebastian picked up a steady pace. He bucked forward, knocking himself in and out of Hugo. The friction of his cock gliding smoothly in and out of Hugo was perfectly tantalising, and it made his insides light with a fire that started at his stomach and spread down his legs in bolts of heat—a sensation that made Hugo wail out loud.

"Ple-aaase. Fucking hell! Please d-don't stop!"

Sebastian chuckled and dug his nails into Hugo's hips. He dragged them down along his flesh, leaving thin red marks blooming across his skin. The sting of pain made Hugo groan in pleasure and he slammed his hips backward. Throwing back his head, he screamed in delight.

Sebastian grabbed Hugo's hips and pulled him back down over the full length of his cock. He hit that sweet spot again and Hugo screamed with joy. Relentless, Sebastian continued to thrust his hips back and forth, repeatedly slamming Hugo down the pole of his shaft, hitting his prostate time after time until his screams became full-fuelled and almost angry with sheer happiness.

"Sebastian!"

His cock twitched and a rope of come shot from the tip of his erection and out across the forest floor. Consumed by exhaustion, he flopped face first against the ground.

With Hugo's muscles tightening around the girth of his cock, it only took a few more heavy thrusts forward before Sebastian's dick was milked of his seed and Hugo was filled with the warm, sticky fluid.

When he pulled out, there was something very satisfying about the slow, hot trickle of it leaking from his now-empty asshole.

"Oh boy," Hugo whispered between heavy pants. He forced himself up onto his knees and then promptly sat down on the forest floor.

Sebastian straightened up and gave Hugo a quick glance over. "What a mess we've made. Those stains are going to take forever to get out."

Six: Lavender & Tea

MUD-CAKED AND RED-FACED, Hugo stumbled like a newborn faun, back to Finchley Hall.

With Sebastian's arm draped around his shoulders, Hugo slumped onto him for support. A dull throb had set into his limbs, and it tingled all the way down to his fingers.

Straining on the forest floor whilst Seb grunted into his ear had really taken it out of him. The kisses that landed across his naked back like butterflies and soft words at his ear afterwards had made up for the rough handling.

"If anybody asks," Hugo began, clearing his throat, attempting to restore some kind of authority over his rogue valet. "I fell into a mud puddle."

Sebastian bit back his smile. "Of course, but hopefully, nobody will even see you returning and we won't have to explain. How about I draw you a bath and get you cleaned up for the day?"

Hugo nodded. That sounded like bliss. He could unwind, knowing that Montgomery would be leaving today and he wouldn't feel obliged to join him for any more late-night drinking.

When they arrived into the hallway, Sebastian crouched down by Hugo.

Hugo took hold of his shoulders for support, and they worked his muddied boots off his feet.

There were no signs that anybody upstairs had risen, and therefore the awkward question of where he'd been and why would not be on a single person's mind.

Sebastian straightened up and touched his shoulder. "How about you go upstairs and wait for me there? I'll take care of your jacket and wellingtons, then be up to fix you a bath."

Hugo nodded dopily in agreement and took the perilous climb upstairs. Once in his room, he unbuttoned his trousers and slipped out of them. His filthy shirt and bow tie followed, and he flopped onto the bed in his underwear and didn't move until Sebastian returned.

When he did, he was armed with the very British remedy of a good cup of tea, A drink that Hugo was learning to love since arriving. Sebastian pressed the cup into his hands and kissed him on the forehead before disappearing to fetch the tub.

The tea filled his tummy with a welcoming warmth and breathed new life into him. Hugo felt quite content to sit on the bed and nurse the cup as if it were a newborn against his chest. The mellow, sweet taste of it on his tongue soothed his senses, and he closed his eyes, allowing himself to relax.

In the background came the sound of the Sebastian bringing in the tub and beginning the gruelling task of filling it. His light footsteps trailed back and forth as he made his way downstairs and back up with another bucket. When he returned a fourth time, the sound of water being sloshed into the bath made Hugo open his eyes.

He fixed Sebastian a look. "You must already be so worn out. You should have just brought me a cloth, and I'd have bathed later." Hugo waved dramatically toward the half-full tub and a clearly exhausted Sebastian. He hadn't minded so much when Edward was tasked with such a mammoth job.

Sebastian rubbed at his forehead with the back of his hand and shrugged. "I don't mind."

Hugo huffed and finished his drink. Sebastian left to haul up the next lot of water.

Waiting for Sebastian to draw his bath, Hugo drifted to sleep until a gentle shake of his shoulder woke him.

"Sir?" Sebastian called, back to formalities at last.

Hugo's eyes drifted apart and he blinked away the sleep. "Is it ready?"

"Yes," Sebastian smiled and moved to stand by the tub with his sleeves rolled up to his elbows. Somehow, he'd managed to remain spotless during their forest tryst. Hugo laughed to himself and rose from the bed, rubbing at his eyes. He stood for a moment, willing himself to wake up, and moved to take off his last remaining article of clothing.

"Ah-ah!" Sebastian interjected, and lifted his hand to make a come-hither motion.

Hugo obliged and crossed the room to stand before him.

Sebastian placed his hands on his bum and gripped a handful of his ass, then gave it a tight squeeze.

Hugo squeaked.

"Hn, sorry...I'm unable to resist," Sebastian purred. His tone sounded anything but apologetic. He hooked his fingers into Hugo's underwear and dragged them down until they fell in a pool at his feet.

His skin was smudged with dirt. Scratch marks criss-crossed over his hips, where fingernails had grazed and dug into the flesh. Beneath his collarbone, a soft bruise had bloomed red and violet. His hair, however, was most impressively ruined. It stood wild, bold and tousled like a caricature, and entwined with dirt and leaves and all kinds of filth.

"This is the first time I've seen your cock and it hasn't been hard," Sebastian mused, biting his lip.

"Shut up."

"Very well." Sebastian held out his arm to help Hugo into the tub.

Hugo stepped over the edge, and when he dipped his toes into the water, he hissed and instantly withdrew his foot. "It's too hot!"

"If you want the aching to stop, this temperature is best. Just brave it and step in. Trust me."

Hugo frowned and took a moment to look from Sebastian down into the steaming tub. Still latched onto Sebastian's arm, he tried again.

He inched his foot back in and gritted his teeth at the fierce sting. This time, however, he kept it in. He took a moment to adjust to the sensation. He wriggled his toes before he decided that Sebastian was right and the water was not going to melt the skin from his bones.

Finally, he plucked up the courage to bring in his second foot. It was the same sensation. A sharp hiss slithered from his mouth, but he forced his foot to stay put. "I've never been in a bath this hot before."

"You'll thank me in a moment," Sebastian reassured him.

At last, Hugo crouched into the bath and slowly, slowly sank into the body of hot water. It rose around him as he sat in the tub. An intense heat rolled across his sore limbs and brought out a near-orgasmic moan of bliss. The water soothed. It seemed to heal his sore muscles almost instantly. Lying back, he let his legs float to the surface, weightless.

Sebastian crouched down beside the tub and fixed Hugo a dashing smile. "I told you."

Hugo rolled his eyes, too elated to argue and simply closed his eyes. "You can get out now."

"And why would I do that?"

Hugo peeked one eye open to see Sebastian hovering mere inches above him, and he groaned. "You're an animal, Seb."

"I'll take that as a compliment." Sebastian seized his jaw. "You're so cute, you're making my dick swell again."

"Seb," he whined. But it was too late. Sebastian kissed him, rough and needy. His tongue rolled over his mouth and forced his lips apart. Hugo closed his eyes and revelled in the sweet, musky taste of their tongues colliding.

Sebastian's hot breath came out in ragged pants, sounds that made Hugo moan against his mouth. Then a sharp sting struck his lips where Sebastian's teeth grazed along his delicate flesh.

At last, Seb pulled back and dropped his hand from Hugo's jaw, leaving a pleasant tingle over his mouth.

Hugo touched two fingers to the spot. "Tease."

Sebastian replied with a flirty smile and sat back a little. He was done.

Hugo sank further into the water, enveloping his body with the warmth. His flesh puckered with goose pimples, drawn out by a simple kiss. The gesture had made a pool of heat bleed into his stomach and his skin tingled with a happy little buzz. Sebastian made it far too easy for Hugo to become aroused. Far too easy for him to submit. Far too willing to give in and surrender to the grinning fox that Sebastian liked to become. If he didn't find his nerve, Sebastian was going to be able to do whatever he wanted to him. Whenever he wanted.

Hugo angled his head right back and rested it on the rim of the bathtub, attempting to ignore Sebastian's looming presence. His cock had stirred again, and it bobbed pleasantly at the surface of the water. He knew Sebastian's attention was on it. He didn't care.

"Let's get you clean first, hm?" Sebastian's voice was right beside his ear.

Hugo nodded dopily, slipped further down in the tub, and plummeted beneath the surface. The water rushed over his head and enveloped him in a bubble of blue. He blew out pockets of air, which rippled up to the surface, and there he stayed, breathless for a few moments.

When he returned, he swallowed in a rush of air. Strands of hair clung to his forehead, soaked.

Sebastian reached toward him to comb his fingers through Hugo's hair and press along his scalp, massaging a lather of shampoo in and washing away the dried dirt.

Once he was done, he dipped something into the water. Light splashing sounds came with a burst of new musky scents. Sandalwood and pine. Something soft and delicate slipped across his arm as Sebastian began to massage the soap into his skin.

The sensation was beautiful. Slippery like silk. Sebastian kneaded the tension from his taut muscles. He worked his fingers in long soothing circles. Attention that brought out delicate purrs of approval from Hugo's mouth.

"Feel's good." He sighed. A stark contrast to only an hour previously, when Sebastian had been rough, and overpowering.

"Good," Sebastian replied and withdrew his hands from Hugo's arms.

Hugo's eyes snapped open in outrage, only to see Sebastian pausing to lather his hands with more soap from the glass bottle.

When he was done, he turned back to Hugo and beamed as their eyes met. Those large hands came back to him. Sebastian reached over the tub to touch his chest and stroke his hands downward in rough stripes. Hugo groaned as the hands wandered across his abdomen, squeezing here and there. The gesture made Hugo squirm, and this only seemed to encourage Sebastian.

He pinched hard at his nipple and chuckled when Hugo squealed. This bath was not as relaxing as he had hoped it would be.

"You're so tense," Sebastian remarked, pausing with his palms flat over Hugo's chest. "You need to relax, sir."

"Tense? Oh, you think?" His cheeks flushed with warmth. Sebastian devoured him with his eyes. His gaze roamed along Hugo's chest and down, into the water and onto his thighs. "Spread your legs."

"What?"

"You heard. Spread your legs, Hugo."

Hugo bit at his lip but obliged and spread his legs apart until his thighs bumped against either side of the tub.

Sebastian lifted a sponge, and Hugo watched him lather it with liquid silk, creating a white slippery foam. Once he was done, he swept it down and began to brush it across Hugo's inner thighs, leaving behind a trail of suds.

Hugo peered up at him, pathetic as a lost cub, with pink cheeks and eyes glassed over with arousal. Sebastian met that expression with a throaty groan. He rolled the sponge between Hugo's legs, careful to avoid getting too close to his semi-erect cock.

Hugo groaned again, longing for Sebastian to grasp at the ache that began to stir between his legs, but he did not oblige. "All done!" Sebastian cried and removed the sponge from the water.

Hugo's eyes flickered open to glare at the offending valet. This bastard didn't know when to call it a day with the teasing.

Hugo made sure to scowl at Sebastian, who simply stood up, expressionless, and grabbed the fresh towel. He held it out toward Hugo. They were done and not once had Sebastian tried to violate him. Hugo couldn't help but feel a touch...disappointed. Keeping his thoughts to himself, he got to his feet and stepped out of the tub, into the welcoming towel.

Sebastian wrapped him up snugly and rubbed his hands down along his towelled arms. "You smell delicious."

"I look it too, I'm sure."

Sebastian smiled in agreement, continuing to rub along Hugo's frame, drying him gently. "You look a little disappointed. May I ask why?"

"I'm fine."

"You'd be more than fine if I—"

"Not now. You ask again and it's back to footman duties you go," Hugo said, smirking.

"Alright, sir, understood."

Hugo smirked and let out a triumphant little hum. "Good. Now, let's not dilly-dally." He wanted to look his best whilst he smugly waved Jacob Montgomery off in a couple hours time. "Do your job, Sebastian Finch, and get me ready."

And so he did.

Seven: Ivory & Crystal

THE ENGLISH SUMMER was certainly nothing to boast about. It was short-lived and mild, with only the occasional bout of blue skies.

It was the end of August, and Hugo glared out of his window at the bleak sky. The sun had been blotted out by black clouds, and a gloomy shadow brewed over Finchley Hall like a bad omen.

Earlier, the sky had been a glorious sapphire and the sun a gold coin. Aunt Ethel had hastily made plans to take Arabella into town to luncheon and light shopping, and Uncle Henry had left to shoot with his friends.

Now, the sun was nowhere to be seen and the clouds were the colour of coal. He hoped it poured and every one of the Harringtons got rained on.

Without a friend to make plans with, Hugo had elected to stay inside and enjoy the peace. To bask in the serenity of an empty house, without the wandering eyes of the Harringtons watching his every move. Without the casual reminder of how ungentlemanly a certain remark he made was or to call him out on his bad manners, like slumping in a heap on the sofa or sitting with his feet propped up against the pouffe.

Still in his pyjamas past noon, Hugo lay in his bedroom, stretched out on his stomach across the cream chaise lounge. Steady hands traced his sketchbook, pencilling the outline of Sebastian's chest from memory. A cigarette dangled limply from his mouth, and he squinted at the page. His copy of *The Gentlemen's Book of Etiquette, and Manual of Politeness,* gifted by Uncle Henry last week, lay unopened on the bedside table beside him.

From downstairs came an outburst of hysterical laughter. Ceaseless and outrageous, it grew in volume and pitch. A second person's laugh entwined with the first, nasal and high-pitched.

Hugo paused his pencil and tipped his head to listen. The laughter continued to ring out from downstairs until it was cut short by a booming voice.

"I've heard enough! Mister Bentley is still home! Control yourselves!" Thompson's voice bellowed, cutting through the laughter that died down into childish sniggers, muffled apologies, and then silence.

Hugo lifted his head. Curious, he sat up, flicked his cigarette into the ashtray, and clambered off the couch.

He wriggled into a rust jumper and pulled it over his pyjama shirt, before venturing barefoot towards the stairs.

He peered over the banister. The two footmen whose names he still hadn't learned after two months were rolling up the Persian rug in the hallway. One had dull blond hair styled like Sebastian's, and the other had dark unruly curls and ivory skin.

Arabella's fair-haired lady's maid with the light blue eyes and rose-lipped smile stood beside them, holding a polished punch bowl.

There was Sebastian too. He stood beside Martha with a vase of chrysanthemum tucked into his arm.

"What's the name of that old fart who always comes?" the dark-haired footman asked, grabbing one end of the rolled rug. The blond grabbed the other and together they lifted it from the floor.

"Narrow it down a bit, George." Sebastian laughed.

"The one with the purple face," George said.

"Oooh, that's Lord Harrison," Martha chimed in.

"Yeah, that's the one." George nodded. "I'm putting my shilling on him. He's always the first to go. Last year, he was chasing pigeons around the garden with his walking stick come nine."

Martha laughed. "Isn't Sam coming? I'd put two shillings on him being drunk first."

"He's usually high, Martha, not drunk," Sebastian said stiffly.

Hugo descended the stairs on his tiptoes. None of them seemed to notice as he crept down and paused on the bottom step. "Are we having a clear-out?"

All heads turned to look his way, alarmed.

Sebastian's gaze swept onto his, and he grinned politely. "No, sir. On the last Saturday of every August, the Harringtons have a summer party. We're clearing space for it."

"Oh." They hadn't told him about this. The Harringtons? A party? The two words were an oxymoron. Hugo snorted his disbelief, rather offended that he hadn't been officially invited to what was likely to be a mess of an event.

Sebastian seemed to notice. "Did nobody mention it?"

Hugo shook his head.

"Excuse us, sir," George grunted. With their conversation about gambling having being overheard, the footmen swiftly began to carry the rug out of the hallway and Martha followed, quick at their heels.

Left alone with Sebastian, Hugo curled his mouth into a smile, unperturbed by the servant's conversation. "A party this evening? If that's the case, I'll be needing some help...picking out an outfit," he purred suggestively and reached out his hand to touch Sebastian's arm.

Sebastian frowned "Sorry, sir, I've been pulled away to help set the house up for this evening. Perhaps later?"

Hugo frowned. "But, it'll only take twenty minutes or so..."

"Sorry..." Sebastian's gaze fluttered over to the door. "I do have to go. I'll see you this evening, we can do it then. Don't pick out anything without me!"

Hugo huffed as Sebastian hurried away. Stuffing his hands into his pockets, he dropped his shoulders and dragged himself into the library instead.

Reading had become one of the few escapes from reality for Hugo. He curled up in the satin wingback like a burrowing animal, surrounded by walls of leather-bound books. Here, where it was quiet but for the repetitive ticking of the mantelpiece clock. Here, undisturbed, where his mind blurred into the adventures written upon pages of crisp beige paper. Here, where time didn't exist. Here, where Hugo grew leaden-eyed and weary and drifted into sleep.

His eyes snapped open and he sat upright with a little snort, alerted by the sudden movement. His book, still open, slid from where it had fallen against his chest. He was met by brown eyes and a rumbling laughter.

"Sir?"

Hugo caught the falling book in his hand and snapped it shut. "Jesus..." he hissed, shifting anxiously in his seat. He dropped the book onto the floor by his feet.

"Hello," Sebastian said and settled his hand over Hugo's inner thigh. He squeezed gently. "You wanted me to help you pick out an outfit?"

Hugo blinked away the sleep from his eyes and gave a lazy nod in response. "You're free now?" he asked, smiling sleepily at Sebastian.

"For a short while, I am," he said, rubbing circles across Hugo's inner thigh. "The house is quiet, and right now, you look so very tempting."

Hugo opened his legs instinctively, and Sebastian moved his hand to Hugo's crotch. He gave Sebastian a pleased noise at the attention and his skin began to prickle. His heart stuttered with excitement at the prospect of getting to play with Sebastian again. Already, yearning for the pleasure that Sebastian's hands could give to him so easily, with a touch here, a stroke there. The heat that would stir in his gut just from the sultry whispers from the man's quivering lips. Sebastian had him entirely at his mercy.

"Sebastian?" a gruff voice called from down the hallway.

Sebastian whipped his head around and wrenched his hand from Hugo's crotch. "Dash it! I have to go. Mister Thompson is pulling out his hair over this party. If he finds out I've been slacking, life will not be worth living." He straightened up.

"But!"

"I know, I'm sorry." Sebastian looked down at Hugo and his expression melted into an apologetic frown.

Hugo pouted, annoyed, but nodded. "Alright, off you go."

Sebastian bowed clumsily and shot out of the library, leaving Hugo alone to sulk at the loss of attention.

BY THE EVENING, Finchley Hall was a changed home. The merry chatter of guests hummed over the modest tinkle of the piano. Soft tame music lit the room with a warm vibrance. A sensible, calming tune soothed like a lullaby through the halls. *O sole Mio.* A pretty piece it was, but a party piece it was not.

Laughter spilled from the immaculately dressed gentlemen. Glasses clinked together in toasts, and when the pianist was done, the guests clapped politely before he began the next soft piece.

In the entrance hall, Hugo lingered. When Sebastian had said the Harringtons were holding a party, this wasn't quite what he had in mind. This evening felt like the opening of an art gallery. Where were the cocktails and the pretty girls with sequins at their hips? Where was the thrash of the saxophone and the quick-stepped dancers? There was no soul, no giddiness, or carefree joy. Only mechanical laughter and sensibilities.

Hugo glared at himself in the hallway mirror, forced a smile at his reflection to check his teeth, and then straightened his back. He was good to go. He took a deep breath and swept into the ballroom to join in with the evening.

His narrowed gaze swept over the clusters of people who gathered together in comfortable circles, chatting. No dancing, no tossing back of alcohol. Soft sips of champagne and pleasant conversation. God, which group to approach first?

"Champagne, sir?"

Hugo whipped his head around and almost squealed in delight at the sight of Sebastian, balancing a drinks tray at the tips of gloved fingers.

"Absolutely! Impeccable timing as always, Seb."

Sebastian floundered into a half smile.

"Save me, Seb. I think I might die here," Hugo groaned as he grasped a fizzing flute.

"You've literally only just stepped through the door, sir..."

"I know but I'm already dying. Please, Sebastian."

"Sir." The valet dipped into a smooth bow and continued on, parading around his drinks platter with pride. Hugo hoped he had some form of plan. He doubted it.

Apprehensively, Hugo scooted toward the first cluster of people to try to break into some form of conversation. In the centre, a man shaped like a globe tooted away at a cigarette. He stood with a man who was the stark opposite in stature—tall, skinny with small eyes—and finally, a very bored young man with a shock of red hair.

"Evening, gents." Hugo sidled up to them and all eyes looked his way. Hugo smiled nervously. He had never been so uncomfortable at a "party" in his entire existence.

The plump man looked toward him, intrigued. "Hello? I haven't seen you around before."

Hugo lifted a hand awkwardly. What a greeting. "Hey. I'm Hugo Bentley. I'm Lady Harrington's nephew," he explained, and his gaze whizzed around the room, trying to spot her. He'd sort of hoped she'd be around to introduce him.

"Aaaah. The infamous Hugo Bentley!"

"Funnily enough, it's not the first time I've been greeted like that." Hugo took a long sip from his champagne.

The redhead stepped forward quite suddenly, threw out his hand, and grasped Hugo's. He was all dimples and freckles, with a charming smile that any fool could see through.

"Hugo! Pleasure! My parents have been talking about how we must meet. New to England, aren't you?" He talked much too fast, and those green eyes were alive with a flame of wicked excitement. He continued to vigorously shake Hugo's hand as he spoke. "I've heard you could use somebody to show you the ropes? Well, I can help there. I know a thing or two about—" He suddenly stopped dead and shot the two older men a wary look as if remembering where he was and cleared his throat. Instead, he gave a throaty chuckle and added, "About England." Whilst giving Hugo a rather ominous wink. "I'm Sam by the way. Say, how about we head out into the garden and have a smoke?" He shot Hugo a pleading look.

"Certai—"

"Hugo!"

Sam's face wrinkled into a frustrated frown.

Hugo looked over to Uncle Henry, who was waving him over with a look of urgency hardening his face.

"Sorry, Sam, we'll catch up in a moment." And hopefully escape into the garden, for Sam seemed like he wanted to be out of this drab excuse for a Saturday night just as much as Hugo did. Hugo was thrilled at the opportunity to mingle with people his own age. Uncle Henry would not ruin this.

Unfortunately, Uncle Henry had other plans. He was very keen on taking Hugo by the shoulder and dragging him around the parlour to introduce him to every single guest.

Mostly, those guests were made up of middle-aged men who had something patronising to say about Hugo and his presence here. It felt rather like being keelhauled through shit. Every glance of disapproval or awkward slap on the back made Hugo's shoulders grow taut.

He suffered through lectures, stories about the war, or comments about how America was awful or great, or about different opportunities and ways in which they thought Hugo ought to spend his time here.

Only a slither of people he met seemed genuinely friendly and only two more seemed as hopeful as Sam. He'd have to wait until Uncle Henry was done before returning to them.

"Dear boy, come and meet your Great-Aunt Gertrude," Uncle Henry said at last and shook his shoulder roughly.

"I'd love to, Uncle. I just…need to go to the gentlemen's and then I shall be right back!" Hugo forced a smile and shot off, bolting for the door before Henry had the time to react.

He needed a moment. Good God, he just needed a short moment to remember that this experience was only for ten more months. All he had to do was play along, pretend to be a changed man, and he would get his trust fund and his inheritance and the entire ordeal would be worth it.

He left through the ballroom doors and scurried up the winding staircase to the next floor. He could hide away for a good thirty minutes before people would start to wonder where he got to. Hopefully by then, Henry would be drunk or occupied enough that Hugo was no longer a concern.

He sped through the corridor, turned the corner, and his hair was seized by a quick hand that grabbed him from nowhere.

Hugo opened his mouth to scream, but the gloved hand smothered the yelp into a muffled groan. Sebastian.

"Going somewhere, are we?" he growled low and feral into his ear.

Hugo's eyes blew wide, and he scrambled to grasp at Sebastian's strong arm. He struggled but was dragged closer so his back pressed up against Sebastian's chest.

Sebastian pulled him backwards, and they disappeared into a cluttered cleaning cupboard.

Once inside, Sebastian snapped the door shut and yanked at the light switch, stunning Hugo into stillness. At last, the gloved hand was removed from his mouth and Hugo gasped his outrage.

"Sebastian! What are you doing?"

Sebastian shoved Hugo's shoulders and knocked him backwards. Hugo stumbled over a leaning mop and slumped against the wall.

"You seemed a little bored," Sebastian said and swept over Hugo to kiss him hard on the mouth.

Hugo's anger melted into a delicate moan, and he relaxed, allowing Sebastian to torment him with his tongue and his hand, which now kneaded circles over his upper thigh.

Hugo closed his eyes and opened his mouth. There was that familiar minty taste, swooping soft damp circles around his tongue. It was a taste Hugo had learned to love. A taste that was always followed by overwhelming pleasure. A taste that made him feel wanted, a taste in which he could forget.

Hugo moaned out his happiness, and together, their lips danced and their chests collided.

Sebastian weaved nimble hands in Hugo's hair again. He clutched a fistful. Sebastian pulled, angling his head back, and kissed Hugo harder.

Hugo responded by spreading his legs further apart. He beckoned for more and Sebastian obliged. His hand wandered up along his thigh and slipped between his legs, massaging hastily at his inner thighs.

Hugo wriggled impatiently until Sebastian groped at his crotch.

When he had asked Sebastian to come up with a plan to get him out of the party, this wasn't quite the response he had been expecting. Perhaps Sebastian helping him to feign sickness or pulling him aside to talk with a very severe expression haunting his face. Yet, here he was, having his cock massaged by a servant, inside a cramped cleaning cupboard. What a funny old time he was having in England.

As Hugo began to purr, the wetness of Sebastian's tongue was removed and he leaned away. Hugo opened his eyes at once.

Sebastian lifted his hand to his mouth and caught the end of his glove between his teeth to pull it off. He lifted the other and did the same before folding them neatly up and slipping them into his pocket.

"Keep those pretty eyes open," he began, catching Hugo's glassy gaze. "I like to look into them when I make you moan." Sebastian reached down the front of Hugo's trousers and grabbed again at his dick.

Hugo's mouth fell open and he moaned. His green stare fixed onto Sebastian's brown. Sebastian's mouth twitched into a predatory smirk, and he rewarded Hugo's obedience by wrapping his hand around the base of his cock.

Quick, generous pumps of his hand rubbed a tingling warmth across his flesh. Then Sebastian seized his cock greedily; squeezing and rubbing at Hugo until waves of pleasure rippled through his dick. They made his body convulse with delight.

"Hnn, you're so good at that," Hugo whined, biting hard at his lip. A heat pooled in his cheeks.

"I know," Sebastian said. He pulled Hugo's trousers to his knees and cupped his testicles. Leaning closer, until they were nose to nose, he mused, "I just love how quickly you get hard for me," and then dipped his head to mouth at the warm flush of his neck.

A series of bites stung over the arch of his throat where his pulse vibrated. Rolling his head to the side, Hugo exposed the valley of his throat to Sebastian's wandering mouth.

Dissolving in the euphoria of Sebastian's touch, he closed his eyes to revel in the sensation.

Those hands were shocking. Sebastian groped, stroked, and squeezed across his cock until all he could feel were intense waves of pure bliss that rolled over every inch of him.

"I'm going to fuck you."

Hugo only moaned out his approval. He wanted Sebastian. He ached for him, for those soft kisses, like electricity across his cold flesh.

Whimpering, Hugo pressed his face into the crook of Sebastian's neck and inhaled. Just the smell of him was enough to arouse his senses. Rich and earthy, like the autumnal air and the lingering scent of cigarette smoke.

It wasn't fair how much Sebastian filled his mind, how often he was taken by the need to be consumed by him. To feel the hollow of his ass being filled by the sheer size of Sebastian's cock.

"Oh God, please," Hugo cried.

Sebastian tugged Hugo's trousers the rest of the way down to his ankles, and Hugo stepped out of them. The moment they were off, Sebastian grabbed him by his hips and spun Hugo around to face the wall.

Hugo pressed his palms to the surface and turned his face to rest against the cold wall. The warmth at his cheeks travelled down to his dick. Sebastian was taking his time behind, and so Hugo began to squirm impatiently.

When he glanced over his shoulder to express his outrage, Sebastian smiled. "You're so needy." He laughed and shoved his hand into his pocket. He pulled out a little round tin and unfastened the top to reveal a pale jelly. He swiped his fingers through it and rubbed his fingers and thumb together, coating them with the slippery substance.

This satisfied Hugo enough, and so he turned back, braced himself against the wall, and stuck out his ass. Despite the earlier excitement, a feeling of nerves bundled up in his gut. His fingers flexed..

"Relax," Sebastian whispered..

Hugo nodded and Sebastian began to press a cold, slippery digit over his opening. He worked slow, teasing circles around the ring of muscle.

Only when Hugo bucked his hips impatiently did he slip it smoothly inside him, knuckle deep, and Hugo let out a sweet moan.

A second one entered Hugo. Sebastian spread his fingers apart and began to thrust them in and out of him in quick pulses. Hugo rolled his head backwards and rested it on Sebastian's shoulder.

Those fingers rubbing along his inner walls released a flurry of joy. They were ripples of pleasure that spiked in his chest and tangled up around his heart, tightening until he was left breathless.

Losing himself, his legs quivered beneath him. "I-I'm going to come."

"Already?" Sebastian sounded appalled. "Jesus."

"I-I'm so sensitive today."

Sebastian swiftly removed his fingers. "We can't have that," he grunted, and from behind the scraping of tin and a satisfying pop could be heard, as Sebastian worked off the lid of his lubricant again. The slippery sound of gel being smeared across flesh made Hugo bristle with excitement.

"Wh-what if somebody hears?" Hugo whispered.

"Moan quietly and they won't," Sebastian said, grabbing hold of Hugo's waist.

He wasted no time. He angled his hips and pressed the tip of his cock against Hugo. For a moment, he teased him, rubbing his length across the line of his crack. The sensation was slick and warm and made Hugo's head reel with anticipation.

Hugo moaned encouragingly, and the girth of Sebastian's cock stretched Hugo's hole apart.

There was a momentary sharp sting when Sebastian pushed his cock up and inside Hugo. He gasped. His toes curled. He was overwhelmed by the sheer size of him.

"F-fuck!"

Sebastian paused, allowing Hugo a moment to relax and adapt to the sensation. "Are you okay?"

It took Hugo a moment, but he nodded at last. His muscles relaxed and Sebastian guided him backwards, pulling him along the length of his cock.

Sebastian groaned out his ecstasy and bucked his hips forward, simultaneously pulling Hugo back toward him.

Hugo glided along his cock, bouncing himself on the length in quick-paced jerks. The angle was incredible, and every time he thrust down Sebastian's cock, a burst of pleasure raged within.

Sebastian slammed against something inside him. Hugo screamed.

Sebastian snarled and aimed for the same spot, slamming against it repeatedly.

It caused a toe-curling pleasure to spring through Hugo like an explosion. "Oh fuck," he yelped, mouth falling open, aghast with how incredible this felt. "Oh God!" His head fell back and the moans continued to pour from his open mouth. "Keep going," he practically squealed with happiness.

"Shush, you're too loud," Sebastian grunted, stern. "How are you so vocal?" He clamped his large hand over Hugo's mouth at once and his breathless moans were muffled. He held it there as his hips rocked against Hugo, and once he was confident Hugo had gotten his yelling under control, he removed it.

"One day, I'm going to do this to you," Hugo whispered, his mouth turning into a twisted grin. He couldn't get enough of the sensation of Sebastian's cock, slipping in and out of him at such a speed. That beautiful friction drove him crazy with need for more. His heart flurried from the effort, his bangs clung to his forehead, his thighs ached from the strain of being pressed up against this wall in such a cramped space, but it was so worth the pain.

Together, their pants and moans melded into a hum of elated sounds, and in a final burst of energy, Sebastian picked up the pace. He slammed himself forward, repeatedly hitting that sensitive spot until Hugo was practically singing his moans.

A warmth squirted up inside his ass. It filled him with a sticky fluid and he gasped with realisation. Sebastian's moans were quiet but feverish in passion. As he came, Sebastian grabbed between Hugo's legs and stroked at his cock, bucking himself into Hugo.

The sensation of being filled with come tipped Hugo over the edge. He shot out a spray of come that splattered up the wall.

Sebastian stroked him through it, until every drop of semen shuddered from his fading erection.

Sebastian leaned forward and kissed Hugo on the head. He pulled his softening cock out of Hugo, and the sensation of Sebastian's come dripping from his hole and down his thighs made him shiver pleasantly.

Hugo's legs wobbled beneath him. With a laugh, he pushed himself away from the wall, turned back towards Sebastian, and pressed his face into his chest. His body still buzzed with post-orgasmic bliss. He felt light and tingly and giddy with happiness.

"My, my...how am I ever supposed to show my face downstairs now?"

Sebastian kissed him again. "Most people are probably too drunk to notice anyway." He reached to pull help Hugo back into his pants before taking care of his own, then produced a spotted red handkerchief from his pocket. "You might want to clean yourself up a bit first, though...uh, and the wall." He pressed it into Hugo's hand and swept in for another kiss before taking a quick step back. "I need to get back to work. I'll see you soon." He shot Hugo one last smile before darting from the cleaning cupboard and out of sight.

The door clicked softly behind him, and Hugo was left to slump onto the wall, dizzy with delight. He supposed this wasn't the *worst* party he'd ever been to.

Eight: Fire & Dust

HUGO LAY SLUMPED against the cold wall of the cleaning cupboard. With his eyes closed and head tilted back, his breaths came out shallow and quick. His legs quivered and his heart wavered. He wondered if sex with Sebastian was always going to leave him feeling like a delicate flower in the wind.

He pressed a hand over his chest and waited in the quiet, with nothing but the sound of his giddy heart throbbing at his temples. How in God's name had he allowed himself to turn into such a damn pushover? England was ruining him, but he sort of...liked it.

Opening his eyes, Hugo lifted his head. He had to pull himself together, before his absence at the party was noticed. He took a deep breath and pushed away from the wall. He could do this. He had to do this...as soon as his face had stopped burning from the shame of being fucked senseless inside a cupboard by his valet.

Frowning, he reached down to fumble with the button of his slacks. He fastened them back, straightened his haphazard bow tie, ruffled his hair back into place, and then, the door of the cupboard was flung open; light from the hall flooded into the cramped space.

Hugo screamed.

Martha screamed too and raised her mop above her head, ready to swing for him. She lurched forward, and then her wide eyes narrowed and her grip on the mop handle went slack. She'd realised who the intruder hiding amongst the cleaning supplies was.

"Mister. Bentley," she gasped. "What are you *doin'*?" She pressed her hand to her chest, her heart racing, no doubt.

Hugo squinted up at her, brow quivering with shame. Quickly, he backed away from Martha, all of two steps until his back hit the dusty shelves behind him. That was a reasonable question. Not one he had a reasonable answer to however.

"Don't be so nosy," he snapped.

"Beg you' pardon, sir, I just—"

"No, I'm sorry." Hugo cleared his throat and straightened his back. He had to address this before she invented her own story. Imagine the gossip downstairs. "I'm hiding from the party."

"Sir?" She leaned the mop against the doorframe and fixed her headpiece, tucking away loose strands of her blonde hair. She really was very pretty.

"I can't stand it down there, Martha. Everybody is so old and dull and tedious. Are all parties in England as dreary as this?"

"Can't say I've been to many me-self, sir."

Something in her tone made Hugo suspect she was lying. He grumbled and stepped out of the cupboard, brushing himself down as he did. If Martha had finished her cleaning ten minutes earlier.... Hugo swallowed thinking about it.

"Surely there's better places to be hidin' than inside a cupboard, sir?"

"I'm sure there are. Right, I'd appreciate it if you uh, didn't say anything to the Harringtons."

Martha beamed and nodded. "Don't think they'd see the funny side of it, sir."

Hugo smiled. "I don't think they would. Sorry to have frightened you." He left her to her work with a wave of his hand.

Descending the stairs, he made sure to grasp hard at the balcony. His legs were still weak, but he had to go back.

He took a good look at himself in the hallway mirror—just in case there were any leftover signs of his tryst—before he returned into the parlour.

There was an old man guffawing in the corner, red faced and teary eyed. He stood, surrounded by a cluster of other men, who'd apparently shared in some sort of joke. Hugo made sure to head in the opposite direction.

"Hugo!" A familiar voice called his name desperately. Hugo tipped his head and spotted the redhead from earlier. He had his arm in the air and waved enthusiastically before jabbing his finger toward two fat cigars in the opposite hand.

God yes. Hugo beamed and hurried through the swarm of people. He made a beeline for Sam before Uncle Henry could catch him in his talons and drag him through the ballroom to meet and greet again.

The moment he was within reaching distance, Sam grabbed his arm and yanked him outside into the sanctuary of the back garden.

White lights wove through the square of groomed hedges, scattered amongst the leaves like a constellation of stars. They lit up the garden with an ethereal, romantic glow.

Stone angels loitered like ghosts in each corner of the hedge square with clasped hands and bowed heads, tall silhouettes with upturned wings against the black night sky.

A cascading fountain, which shimmered as it caught the light, trickled away in the centre of the garden. Silver water spilled over the curved edges of the three-tiered design, as soft as a lullaby. It offered peace and serenity from the hustle and bustle of the party.

Though it was the smallest, this garden was their gardener's pride and joy. Under the sunlight, flowers scattered across their beds like confetti. Purple lavender was tucked away beneath the shuttered windows in marble planters, and sunflowers stood tall, lined up one by one against the red brick wall.

Sam sat down on a marble bench and crossed his legs. He cocked back his head and offered Hugo a debonair smile so big it dimpled his freckled cheeks. He held out a cigar toward Hugo, who plucked it from his fingers with a grateful word of thanks.

"Thank God you're here," Hugo huffed, rolling the cigar between his finger and thumb. He perched himself on the edge of the bench beside Sam and put the cigar to his mouth.

"Right?" Sam laughed, sparking up a lighter, he turned his cigar in his fingers and held the flame to the tip, beginning the process of lighting it. After it was glowing, he lifted it to his mouth and puffed, bringing the lighter up once again. Once satisfied, he handed it over.

"I hate coming here," Sam began. "My parents always insist. They think I might get with one of these dull girls." He snorted. "I have to keep them happy, so I come. But obviously, this isn't my usual scene." He mouthed at the cigar, his shoulders tense, and he leaned back against the hedge. "I need to take you to a real party, what do you say?"

Hugo sat forward, eyeing Sam. His mouth twitched into a smile. "I'm supposed to be grounded from things like that."

"Oh, come off it," Sam spat. Whenever he took a drag from his cigar, the corners of his eyes crinkled. He squinted at Hugo, "It's not like anyone'd find out. You think my parents approve of the parties I like to go to? Not a chance."

Hugo hesitated, his fingers curled around his still unlit cigar. "If they were to find out..." He threw an awkward look back at the house.

"They won't," Sam reassured him softly. He reached out his bony hand and patted Hugo hard on the shoulder. "What kind of parties do you like? Ones with jazz? With drugs, with...women? If you know what I mean..." His mouth lifted into a sloppy smirk.

Hugo tried to relax a little. He crossed his legs and finally sparked up the lighter to ignite his cigar. He puffed quickly at it, sucking the rich, sharp flavour into his lungs. It sent a wave of calm sweeping through him at once.

"All of the above," Hugo replied easily.

"I think you and I will get along rather nicely, Hugo." Sam laughed.

Hugo grinned. He hadn't met anybody quite like Sam here. He was an awful lot like his friends back home.

The Harringtons had tried to introduce him to a couple of young men who were okay but didn't quite know how to have a good time. He needed somebody like Sam. Somebody easygoing, somebody he didn't need to watch himself around. Somebody willing to accompany him to a jazz bar, where he could throw himself around against a backdrop of smoke and saxophones and forget he was cooped up in England. Hugo just needed to let loose in other ways than those that Sebastian afforded him.

The two of them talked about the sorts of trouble they'd gotten themselves into in the past, their aspirations, and their dreams. They spoke of ideal women, their favourite sports. They were both simply able to enjoy each other's company and be themselves without fear of judgement. Hugo felt liberated...until the silhouette of a tall man appeared, pacing down the steps that led into the garden. Hugo recognised his frame instantly.

"Sir?" Sebastian came into view and paused at the foot of steps with his hands stuffed into his pockets. He looked exhausted. His weary gaze was on Sam. "Your father has been searching for you for twenty minutes." By the look on his face, he meant *he* had been. Sam's father was inside, drunk on wine with a belly full of food, no doubt.

Sam looked outraged. His face hardened into a severe line and his freckled cheeks puffed out. He stood from the bench with an exaggerated groan. "For goodness sake, what does he want?"

"Of that, I am not entirely sure, sir. Perhaps your family is due to leave."

"Absolutely ridiculous. It's not even late." Sam shook his head and turned to look at Hugo. "I'll see you soon. Saturday second." He shot him a wink before hurrying inside to seek his father.

Sebastian hovered a moment. He looked over Hugo and smiled before turning his back.

"Seb! Sebastian...talk with me?"

Sebastian hesitated and turned to look back at him. "I have to help clear up."

"When you're finished?"

"When I'm finished."

QUIET HAD FALLEN over Finchley Hall at last. The hour was late, and one by one, the lights upstairs were flickering off. Hugo was still sitting on the bench. He leaned against the hedge with his arms folded, enjoying the peace and quiet.

The cool air soothed his skin—a breeze that no longer held the pleasant warmth of summer. It had a cold touch that whispered up his sleeves and kissed goose bumps across his arms. If he sat out here for too much longer, he knew he would start to shiver.

At last, Sebastian reappeared in the garden, still in his uniform with the addition of a navy wool scarf coiled around his neck. Hugo looked up and smiled.

"Did you have a good night, sir?" Sebastian asked. He wandered past Hugo, though, and disappeared around the back of the hedge walls, out of sight from any wandering eyes, without a word of explanation.

Hugo spun around in his seat, watching Sebastian venture past, and he rose from the bench at once. What on earth was he up to this time?

Hugo rolled his eyes, but unable to help himself, he followed Sebastian like a lost puppy.

"A very good night, thanks to you...and Sam," he answered quickly, then caught up with Sebastian and followed him around the bushes.

Sebastian stopped suddenly and turned around to face Hugo.

Hugo stopped before him and tilted his head back to look Sebastian in the eyes, his own crinkled with pure happiness. They stood with their chests pressed together.

Sebastian smiled and reached down to ruffle Hugo's hair. "I'm glad. Though, sir, you must know, Sam is notorious for getting himself into trouble..."

"So am I!"

"Exactly my point." He sighed, brow wrinkling. "I don't want you to be bad influences on each other. I mean, I know it's not my business. I'm just saying—be careful."

Hugo nodded and took a slight step back from Sebastian, eager to move on the subject. "I do wish we could spend more time together. You're supposed to be my valet, but Thompson is always finding ways to snatch you up from me."

Sebastian jeered, snorting in disbelief. "You sound like a jealous lover."

"I like spending time with you."

Sebastian frowned a touch. "And I do too, but we have to be careful. You know we could go to jail for this, right?" Despite himself, Sebastian took Hugo's hands into his own. He lifted them to his mouth and planted a soft kiss to the backs of them.

Hugo nodded. His gaze moved to stare at the floor. "I know."

Sebastian began to work his thumbs in circles across Hugo's hands. "Now the summer is over, things will calm down, and you'll have me all to yourself—at least, until the festive season begins."

"Hmm, good." It took a lot not to nuzzle into Sebastian, not to steal a quick kiss from those tempting lips. This was already dangerous enough.

The wind was beginning to pick up by now, and a shiver of it fluttered through the collar of his shirt and hissed down his spine. Hugo trembled. His hands clenched at Sebastian's and he drew up his shoulders.

"You're cold," Sebastian said, almost accusingly.

"'M fine."

Sebastian dropped his hands and began to uncoil the wool scarf from around his neck. He slipped it around Hugo's instead. It was soft and still warm.

"You should know better than to lie to me. I can read you like a book," he said affectionately as he began to knot it in place around Hugo's neck.

Hugo almost melted at the sweetness of the gesture. Grinning like an idiot, he pulled the scarf tighter around his neck and lifted the material to his nose. It smelled like him too. "Thanks."

"You're welcome. Now, come, let's get you inside, I'm absolutely exhausted." He kissed him on the cheek. "I'll bring you up some hot chocolate."

Hugo nodded in agreement, feeling for the first time in a while he would get a decent night of sleep.

Nine: Rum & Jazz

AUNT ETHEL KISSED Hugo on both cheeks. "I'm sorry you're feeling rotten, darling. Charles will drive you back home and you go straight to bed." Her delicate hand patted his cheek.

Hugo managed a wobbly smile and leaned against the back seat. "I'm sorry I'm not feeling up to dinner. Do send my sincerest apologies to the Coupe family." Hugo's voice was feeble. With trembling shoulders and heavy eyes, he probably looked a meek, pathetic creature, ready to burrow beneath the ground and hide away from the sunlight.

"Seems like nothing more than a little car sickness, Hugo," Uncle Henry grunted, mouthing at the end of a cigar. Ethel nudged him.

"I've felt terrible all day," Hugo huffed, slouching further down. It took a lot of willpower not to glare at Henry and his cold expression.

Uncle Henry pulled the cigar from his lips and a cloud of smoke barrelled from his mouth. "Get home, lad. We'll see you in the morning." He tapped the boot of the convertible, then leaned over the edge of the car to talk to the chauffer "Take him home, Charles. If he's in no fit state to walk, you call for Sebastian."

"Understood, sir," Charles replied, and with that, the tyres crunched and they rolled forward.

The Harringtons stood at the end of the Coupe's grand drive and waved Hugo off until they were no longer in sight.

The chauffeur was a stoic man, with the face of a mouse and waves of brown curls that he struggled to manoeuvre into an orderly fashion. He was not a big talker. The only communication he seemed to make was the occasional flash of those brown eyes meeting Hugo's via the rear-view mirror.

The sun was beginning to set behind them, stealing away the blue sky with it. Hugo leaned forward and rested his elbows on back of the driver's seat. The wind whispered through his hair, which billowed in waves about his head. It ticked along his spine and made him smile.

"We're not going home."

"Sir?" Charles's brows knitted together.

"You think I wanted to sit through another dinner and discuss politics? Not a damn chance. I'd rather bury myself alive. No, we're going to pick up my friend Sam, and then you're going to drive us into town."

Charles groaned. "I was told to take you home."

"Technically, you are taking me home. We're just going to take a little detour first."

"I don't think—"

"And I will pay you kindly for the extra hours of work and for the awkward position I have put you in."

Charles's grasp tightened around the steering wheel, but he nodded. "Very well, sir." And with that, the deed was done.

They parked up at the corner of George Avenue, and there, they waited for Sam beneath the glow of a street lamp. Hugo heard the man before he saw him. Delighted and perhaps already a little intoxicated, his cry of greeting cut through the air. Then, his lanky silhouette appeared from out of the darkness. He had one arm raised above his head and waved it at Hugo.

He'd missed Sam and his charming smile. Sam was the type that used money as a weapon and as an excuse for his reckless behaviour. Hugo bet he could pay his way out of anything.

Suited up in his best tuxedo, with his red hair slicked back and debonair smile ever-present, he yanked open the car door and scrambled clumsily into the vehicle. "Well, hello there, Hugo," he cried in his best mock American accent.

Sam slammed the door shut and wriggled across the back seat until he was pressed up tight against Hugo. His long arms wrapped around his shoulders as the car began to pull away from the pavement.

"Sam, you look grand," Hugo mused, his green eyes fluttered over his attire with an impressed cock of his brow. Even the forceful whip of the wind rolling over them wasn't enough to tarnish Sam's slicked-back hair.

"Thanks." He tugged gently at Hugo's jacket sleeve. "I see you didn't fancy a tuxedo for a jazz lounge? I don't blame you, entirely inappropriate. However, I do like to meet certain standards."

"Well, I was going to wear burgundy velvet." Hugo edged ever so slightly away from Sam, creating more room between their compacted bodies.

"Then why didn't you?"

"My valet was having none of it." Also, he'd told Sebastian he was going to a dinner party at the Coupe's.

"Ah? And he's in charge of you, is he?"

Hugo smiled crookedly. "Something like that."

There was an overwhelming stench of something rich and earthy radiating off Sam, an infusion of dirt and herbs that made Hugo feel a little light-headed. The smell only became more powerful as the car picked up speed. They flew down the high street. Hugo's ears buzzed with the rush of the passing scenery.

Hugo tipped his head and cast Sam a curious look.

Sam's eyes met his again. "What's up?"

"Have you been smoking?"

Sam's mouth shivered into a grin. He reached into the inner pocket of his jacket and produced a fat handmade roll-up, stuffed with a green herb and tobacco. "Would you care for a smoke, darling Hugo?"

Hugo took it and held it under his nose. He gave it a long sniff and his eyes widened. Sam's lighter flared orange, and he held it out. Without hesitation, Hugo stuck the butt of the joint between his teeth...

BY THE TIME they pulled up to the main square, where music pulsed through the streets and rolled over their skin with the breeze, Hugo's head felt like it had been stuffed with feathers. His body weighed ten pounds lighter and his world had been painted over in light pastels and yellows. In his chest, his heart sang happily and his skin prickled with energy.

It took the help of Charles's gloved hands to lift him from the car. The moment he was on two feet, a childlike laughter stirred in his belly, and he found himself giggling against the palm of his hand.

"Have a good evening," Charles retorted through gritted teeth. With that, Sam grabbed Hugo by the arm and pulled him hastily through the square and in the direction of the bubbling jazz.

Together, they ventured into the lounge, where the air was heavy with silver smoke and musky with the smells of nicotine, cheap perfume, and sweat.

Girls danced with their hips, arms raised to the air. They threw back their heads and giggled mindlessly, purely intoxicated by liquor. Beneath the dim lights, their jewelled headpieces and sequined dresses glinted and threw scattered light across the ceiling.

Sam slipped a hand into Hugo's and locked their fingers together. The rhythmic thump of the saxophone spilled out across the room in drunken toots. In the background came the clash of the symbols and a tinkle of the skilled pianist's dainty fingers. Feet tapped, fingers clicked, and men and women swirled together, knocking their hips and locking arms. It was tasteless romance. Hugo loved it.

He smiled and leaned into Sam, who opened his arms to his friend and wrapped them around his shoulders. Together, they swayed over by the corner of the dance floor, where the pools of low light did not quite touch them.

"You're a mess," Sam mused, his breath hot against Hugo's ear.

Glassy eyed, Hugo lifted his gaze to look at his friend. "Hmmm? And whose fault is that?"

"Hey, I only offered. You could have refused."

Hugo laughed again and threw his arms up into the air. He allowed the music to take hold of him. To rattle down into his inner core as he danced.

Sam let out a bark of laughter as he watched his friend let loose. "You are a sloppy mess, Mister Bentley!" He shook his head and lifted a hand to smooth back his already perfect hair. "Here, I have something that will help." He gestured Hugo closer.

Hugo looked up, curious.

"After this, you'll dance the Charleston all night long."

"What is it?" Hugo asked, his words slow and soft.

Sam took Hugo by the hand and dragged him over to a dark corner of the club. There, he dusted the table with soft white powder. He lovingly arranged it with an ace of hearts into two perfectly neat lines. Once he was done, Sam raised the card to his mouth and licked off the dusting as if it was icing sugar. He flashed Hugo a playful smile and from within his pocket, produced a one-pound note and rolled it tightly into a tube. Sam stuck the end of the note into his nostril and bowed his head to snort, when he lifted it again, a line was gone.

"Your turn." Sam flipped the note the over and pushed it into Hugo's hand.

Hugo pressed the rolled-up note into his nose and lowered his head. He sniffed. A sharp burn stung inside his nose, and his body was consumed by overwhelming bliss that prickled over his skin like electricity. An inferno had been lit within him and his night turned into an exhilarating rush of energy that he released in a jagged uncontrollable dancing. He and Sam howled with laughter as they spun together and spilled rum down the front of their fancy suits.

They stood chest to chest and their mouths pressed together, sloppy, wet, thrilling.

They twirled with girls and ended up with bright lipstick smeared across their cheeks. They passed cigars around circles of babbling men, and Hugo hacked up his lungs from laughing whilst inhaling the toxic fumes into his body.

He knocked back gin and honey cocktails until his throat was numb. He drank champagne and whisky and cognac until his stomach churned and his mouth watered in protest. He drank until he could barely hold himself upright. The coursing of his quickened heart rate caused his breath to be ragged and panicked. He staggered from the club for a little fresh air and slumped against the outside wall. Everything went black.

"SIR? SIR!" A distant voice echoed inside his head. It rattled around behind his eye sockets and urged him to wake. It was a terrified voice that Hugo did not quite recognise. Something was wrong.

Rousing from his drug-leaden slumber, he groaned.

Strong hands grasped his shoulders and shook him.

His eyes flew apart, and he was greeted by the sight of his chauffeur, kneeling beside him in the dirt. Hugo stared up at the man, whose figure seemed to ripple like a heatwave in the savannah. Why was Charles here?

Charles was silhouetted against a sky that was turning a dusky blue. His shoulders were hunched high and his hair was more untamed than Hugo had ever seen it. "Sir!"

Hugo squinted at him, his nose wrinkled, waiting for the man to give him some kind of answer, for he could not find the energy to make words.

Charles looked like a rumpled ghost; those mousey eyes were filled with pure overarching fear. They were wild with it as he continued to shake Hugo. "Sir," he gasped again.

"I'm up, I'm up..." Hugo muttered. God, it *hurt* to talk. Acid and bile hissed in his throat, staining his tongue with a metallic bitterness. Saliva gathered in his mouth, but he forced it down. He was going to be sick.

"Hugo," Charles snapped in a tone that brought Hugo back to his senses. Stunned, he looked to the chauffeur and began to realise just how wrong this situation was.

He was wet. *Why was he wet?* Hugo reached behind him and felt at the soggy patch on his shirt. His back was soaked, his bum too. Beneath him, the ground was soft and damp, and he suddenly realised he had been lying, asleep in a field. His socked feet pressed into a muddy puddle, shoeless. His jacket was nowhere in sight either.

"I am in so much trouble! I was supposed to be at the Coupe's to pick up your family four hours ago," Charles wailed, his hands still clutching at Hugo's shirt.

"Shit," Hugo groaned, sitting up. The movement caused his stomach to convulse into a hurricane of fire. Flames licked their wicked tongues along the lining of his stomach, and he whimpered. He pulled his legs up into his chest and rested his chin in the gap between his knees.

He attempted to piece together thoughts and memories that would point to how he had got here, wherever here was. Where was Sam? Where were his shoes? His head reeled.

"Please, sir. We have to go!" Charles tugged at Hugo's sleeve, and finally, with some help, Hugo pulled himself off the ground and staggered to his feet, clearly still intoxicated.

With jellyfish limbs, he was dragged, mostly, toward the car. Charles yanked open the door and pushed Hugo inside. He fell, head first onto the back seat, and there he lay, drooling against the nice, clean leather.

His head lolled from side to side with the bumpy movements of the car ambling over the field, but he didn't move for the entire journey back.

THE HALLWAY WINDOW was still illuminated when they pulled up at Finchley Hall. Hugo's gut churned. Somebody had waited up.

The engine was snuffed out, and Charles bolted around to the passenger door. He hastily pulled it open, but Hugo did not move.

"I absolutely must leave, sir. To pick up your family," he said stiffly.

Hugo nodded dopily. He still did not move. His chest was growing tighter, and his breaths became trapped in his throat. His lungs ached with the strain of trying to keep his breaths even and steady.

The consequences of what he'd dared to do tonight winded him. Charles would lose his job. That poor hectic-faced chauffeur. Hugo noticed it now as he wove his hands frantically, gesturing for him to get out of the car. A silver wedding band. Tonight, he'd be out of a job. He'd be unable to support his family...all because Hugo had been reckless.

Hugo braced himself on the door, grabbed at Charles's arm, and hauled himself out of the car at last. Collapsing against Charles's shoulder, his face crumpled. "I'm sorry," he whispered.

The nausea was worse than ever now. It bubbled up in his chest, made his heart balloon and rise up into his throat. The swollen mass would not give up. "Listen, Charles," he began.

Charles turned his gaze down to look at Hugo and grimaced.

"I'm going to cover for you. T-Tell them I told you to stop b-because I was going to be sick. When I got out, I disappeared into the bushes and didn't come back." He was still inundated with toxins, but his mind, accelerated by shock, had begun to piece back together his wits.

"Your aunt and uncle will not forgive you easily for this, sir," Charles said, relief in his voice. He would not take the fall, despite his part in allowing it to happen.

"I don't have a job on the line, Charles—you do."

Perhaps this would be the end for him. He'd be cut off from the family. Sent back home to America with a very small allowance where he would have to set up a middle-class life, working.

"Let's get you inside," Charles said, his tone gentler now. He took hold of Hugo's arm and led him up the steps and to the front door, where Charles tapped the great lion's head knocker.

After a matter of seconds, the door was pulled open to floods of yellow light. A hard-faced Thompson greeted them. His mouth a haggard line, his eyes a picture of pure anger. He turned his gaze onto Charles.

"What in heaven's name do you call this, Charles? We have been in fits of panic!"

"Mister Thompson, I—"

"Lord Harrington calls to say Mister Bentley is on his way, he doesn't show. You don't show to pick them up. By God almighty, you have some explaining to do." He turned to Hugo then, looking him over in disdain.

Hugo wondered what sort of state he must look. All dirtied up and without his shoes.

Charles's mouth flopped open.

"Mister Thompson," Hugo grunted. "It's all my doing. But, please, not now. I need to go to bed before I pass out. I'll explain the morning."

Thompson grumbled, outraged. His cheeks were red and puffy. "Very well," he snapped, disgusted by what he was seeing, but he held no authority to demand anything of Hugo in his current state and he knew it.

"Get to bed. I will call your family to let them know you are safe. They will return tomorrow; the Coupes have kindly offered them a place to stay. They have the police on the case by now, I'm certain."

Incapable of giving much more of a response, Hugo bobbed his head in some form of haphazard agreement. Wriggling out of Charles's grasp, he shuffled toward the staircase.

A figure lingered on the steps.

He stood with his mouth turned in a scowl. Dark hair unruly about his head and his hands stuffed into the pockets of his patchwork dressing gown. "You're okay?" he asked curtly.

Hugo nodded, unable to look Sebastian in the eye.

Satisfied enough with that response, Sebastian stepped down the final steps and swept toward Hugo. Without a word, he wrapped his arm around Hugo's frame and aided Hugo in climbing the stairs.

Hugo was rigid as he went. He was waiting for Sebastian's wrath to come raining down on him, for the angry words, to be reprimanded for being reckless, yet again.

Sebastian radiated anger. He could see it in the stiff way he held himself, in the way his mouth remained a hard unmoving line. It was in the absence of eye contact between the two, no matter how desperately Hugo sought it.

Carelessly taking the last step up, Hugo lost his balance. He jolted forward, but Sebastian tightened his firm grip and pulled him upright before he hit the steps.

"Thanks..." Hugo said, and clung tighter onto Sebastian's arm.

Sebastian sighed.

They continued until they were safely back into his bedroom, where Hugo fell on the bed and lay sprawled out on his back. The world spun on its head and drifted together in a smear of colour.

Beneath him, the mattress melted and his limbs weighed like lead.

Hugo scrunched his eyes closed, blotting out the chaos, but the sensation only intensified.

In the background, Sebastian meandered about the room. His footsteps echoed, light, authoritative. He stopped beside the bed, and then, there was a gentle tugging at his wet socks. No question about his lack of shoes.

Familiar hands flicked across his waistband and his trousers loosened. Sebastian grabbed the hems of his slacks and worked them down his legs with alternate tugs, careful not to let his hands linger anywhere for a moment too long.

Once his trousers were off, Hugo peeked one eye open. He sneaked Sebastian an anxious look. His expression was hard and focused, and those beautiful eyes refused to look Hugo's way. His shoulders were drawn up high, and a stray hair hung loosely over his forehead.

"Sebastian?" he tried.

"Sir?"

"Are you angry with me?"

"It's not my place to be angry with you, sir," he said coldly, and reached down and began to unbutton Hugo's shirt.

Hugo frowned. Not his place?

Sebastian had challenged him many times in the past. What was he getting at? Hugo wanted to ask, but his words became lost in his parched throat. Perhaps now was not the best time to broach the topic. Instead, an insufferable silence smothered the room but for the snapping of the shirt buttons as Sebastian worked his nimble hands along them.

At last, Sebastian finished the painful process. He slipped it off and threw it over his arm with Hugo's dirtied slacks.

"Should I help you into your nightwear, sir?" he offered.

"No, no," Hugo said a little too quickly. "Ah...n-no, get yourself to bed, Sebastian. I-I'll see you tomorrow."

"Very well, sir." And with that, he left, turning out the light as he went. The door clicked softly behind him and the room was thrown into complete darkness.

Hugo leaned back into his pillows and absorbed the bitter loneliness of silence. Here, he would lie awake and contemplate just how much damage he had done.

Ten: Silence & Serenity

LIGHT-HEADED, WITH SWEATY palms and his bangs clinging to his forehead, Hugo paced his room. It was the next morning. His curtains were pulled tight over the window to shut out any stray beams of light entering his room. It was dark and stuffy and smelled like musk, sweat, and alcohol.

As he paced across the floor, his legs quivered beneath him, as if the floor was trying to suck him under and swallow him whole. Hugo wished it would. It'd be a damn lot easier than having to deal with Uncle Henry. The man still hadn't summoned for him yet. Perhaps he wasn't back from the Coupe's.

Hugo groaned and paused his frantic pacing. The floor rippled beneath him like water and the bedroom walls seemed to sink slowly.

He squeezed his eyes shut and pinched the bridge of his nose, trying to will away the dizziness that swept through him. He ought to sit down, but he was sick of sitting, waiting like a fat duck during open season.

Perhaps the dizziness would subside if he just had something to eat. Hollow and wilting, his stomach cried, but he could not will himself to call for Sebastian. Perhaps he could sneak downstairs and get breakfast himself? Perhaps he was already in too much trouble to try to pull a stunt like that, but his throat felt like an hourglass. He at least needed some water.

Hugo made a gurgling sound in the back of his throat. It was too damn stuffy in here. He hooked a finger into the collar of his dressing gown and loosened it. Perhaps he was dying.

What was the time? He whipped his head around to look to the bedside table and began to hobble over. Fumbling, he managed to yank open the drawer and slip his hand inside. Feeling about, he brushed the chain of his timepiece, then pulled out the copper watch, etched with intricate leafy tendrils that swirled across the cover.

He opened it up to take a quick look. Ten thirty-two. Well, no wonder he was starving. Why on earth had Sebastian not been to call on him? Even to check if he was still alive? Hugo dropped the heirloom back into his drawer and slammed it shut.

Scoffing, he careened over his bed and grabbed the bell pull. He tugged, five times and fell, face first, into a heap on the bed. There, he lay until there was a rapping at his door.

Hugo didn't have the time to answer the knock. The door was hurled open anyway and the familiar fall of Sebastian's footsteps came from behind.

"Are the Harringtons back?" Hugo sighed against the fabric of his pillow.

"Charles is picking them up in ten minutes. They'll be here for luncheon," Sebastian answered flatly. His tone free from the cheerful ring it usually had. Even without looking, Hugo could tell there was no smile on his face.

Hugo wriggled a little. That's why he hadn't been summoned, then—not because Uncle Henry was delaying the talk as a means of torture. At least he could eat in peace without worrying about being interrupted by a hysterical old man.

Slowly, he lifted himself away from the mattress and rolled over to sit on his behind. He rubbed at his eyes and threw a look at the breakfast tray. He made a disgusted sound in his throat.

"Toast and tea? Is this some kind of joke?"

"Do I look like I'm in the mood to be playing jokes?" Sebastian asked curtly.

Hugo dragged his gaze over to him. Sebastian stood close to the door, stiff and scowling. He certainly didn't.

Sebastian sighed and shifted awkwardly. "Thompson's orders. You clearly weren't just drunk last night. Don't think I didn't see the cocaine powder you had all down your trousers. I think your body will appreciate the simplicity of it."

"I feel like I'm being punished."

"It's not a very good punishment for what you did if that's the case."

"Oh God. Not you too, Sebastian." Hugo heaved out a dramatic sigh and rolled his eyes. He shifted a little and crossed his legs. He wasn't going to sit and allow Sebastian to lecture him. He had no business in it. He folded his arms over his chest and looked away.

"I'm not sorry for being upset with you over this."

"Of course you're not." Hugo sighed.

"You were reckless."

Hugo whipped his head around to glare at his valet. "That's what I am! *Reckless!*" Why was Sebastian being so difficult? Valets were not supposed to pass judgement on their masters. They certainly were not supposed to take sides and belittle them. Sebastian should be here, taking care of him whilst he was down and sick.

Instead, he let out a bark of laughter. A cruel sound, that. A taunting sound that made Hugo's cheeks flare with heat. A spark flared in his chest and blew up within him, it made his skin prickle and his heart shatter in betrayal.

"That's not an excuse," Sebastian said. "You were stupid! If you continue behaving like this, you're going to lose everything and I wo—"

"Don't you *dare* lecture me, Finch," Hugo snapped, stopping Sebastian in his tracks. "You're *nothing* but a cocky, arrogant man who gets off on telling others what to do." He stood up from the bed.

"I beg your pardon?" Sebastian looked rather taken aback.

"You heard."

"I'm staggered by how immature you're being." Sebastian frowned and his brow creased into a deep-ridged wrinkle.

"Fuck off, Sebastian!"

Sebastian cocked a brow. His mouth twitched as if he were about to say something...but he didn't. Those beautiful eyes seemed to darken, though, and he reached behind him to touch the doorknob.

"Will that be all, sir?"

Hugo glowered. "No. That will not be all. I'm the one who dismisses you. Don't you *dare* open that door." Hugo took a step forward.

Sebastian released the handle and dropped his arm back to his side. He pressed his lips together.

"That's right," Hugo snarled. He drew up his shoulders and clenched his fist tightly at his side, then crossed the room to confront him.

Hugo stood before Sebastian and tipped back his head to glare up at him. "Remember your place, Finch."

"Sir, I—"

"Stop talking," Hugo said, his breathing picking up. He leaned closer to him so they were nose to nose, and the room began to spin. "You're just a valet, Finch. A self-righteous, self-loving, manipulative piece of shit. You're *nothing*. That's why you do nothing but serve other people." Hugo kicked at the door behind Sebastian, who flinched. "Go. Get out. If even you won't defend me from this hellhole, get fucked!"

Sebastian dipped into a graceful bow and with red shame-tinged cheeks, he bolted from the room.

HUGO SAT, HUNCHED on the bed, and nibbled the end of a slice of, by now, cold, soggy toast swamped in butter. His feet swung to and fro whilst he tried to keep down the mountain that had begun to rise from within his chest and grow up into his throat.

Why did he have to be such a damn child? Losing his temper like that, saying such aggressive, terrible things to the only person who'd been something of a friend here.

It didn't matter. This was probably his last day at Finchley Hall.

He cursed between mouthfuls and lifted a hand to wipe away tears.

WHEN UNCLE HENRY did finally call on him, Hugo had managed to somewhat pull himself together. He'd washed and slipped into some casual house wear, which, by Harrington standards, consisted of cream slacks, an ivory button-down, and a red velvet waistcoat.

With his head bowed, he headed downstairs with his hands stuffed into his pockets and a guilty expression on his face. Martha passed him in the hall and gave him a wary look when she didn't think he was looking.

Hugo sighed. God, he really hated this place. He turned onto the next corridor, headed for the blue room, but slowed when he heard voices.

"Mister Bentley said he was going to vomit, sir." It was Charles. He sounded like a mouse trapped in the claws of a cat. Hugo could bet he was trembling, for the job he loved was quite possibly about to be taken from him.

Hugo waited outside the door, unsure if he should knock...or continue to eavesdrop.

"He clambered out of the car and assured me he'd only be five minutes, needed the fresh air, you see. Perhaps to grab a tea from the café just over the road, soothe his stomach. However, when Mister

Bentley still hadn't returned after almost an hour, I got very concerned and headed across to see if he was okay. Unfortunately, Mister Bentley was not there."

Henry huffed. Charles continued.

"The lady told me he'd got talking to a group of young men. They'd headed across to the pub for a quick drink."

"Oh for goodness sake," Henry snarled, incredulous.

"S-so...I began to wander between the pubs, looking for him. I supposed he must have been feeling better. Sir, don't you think you ought to hear the rest from Mister Bentley?"

"Absolutely not! Carry on, Charles!"

"Well." He swallowed. "By the sounds of it, he did only intend to stay for a quick drink and then come back. Unfortunately, Mister Bentley did not have his wits about him. They put something in his drink, and then they took him away and mugged him."

Henry sighed. "You believed this codswallop story?"

"Well, sir, when I found him, he was unconscious. He had no wallet, no shoes, and no jacket. It seemed to add up."

"He was unconscious?"

Silence. Hugo assumed Charles nodded.

"He's a damn fool, Charles. A damn fool. He's lucky he's alive," he spat.

Hugo heaved out a sigh of relief. Thank goodness for Charles and his heroism. He reached out finally and tapped on the door.

"You'd better come in, Hugo. Charles, you are not deserving of disciplinary action. This is all my blasted nephew's fault."

"Sir."

Cautiously, Hugo pushed the door open and stepped into the room. He hovered awkwardly by the door and tried a sort of nervous half smile at his uncle, who only scowled in return.

"Sit."

Hugo scuttled forward and sat, stiff as a board in an armchair.

As soon as the door clicked behind Charles, Henry began. He stood with his back to the grand fireplace, his hands stuffed into his pockets. "Boy, you are on your final warning."

"I quite understand, Uncle Henry."

"Oh no, I don't think you do," he answered, his moustache twitching. "I mean it. Another peep out of you and you are done for. I won't give a damn what happens to you after that."

Hugo sunk lower into his chair. "Sir, I didn't mean for this to happen."

"It would not have happened if you didn't wander off with some riff-raff! Charles was supposed to take you home. He almost lost his job because of your little stunt." He narrowed his eyes until they became wrinkled slits.

Hugo didn't know what to say. Perhaps it was best to simply allow Henry to finish.

His uncle continued on, pacing now, his cheeks becoming redder as he spoke. "You need to start associating yourself with some *real* gentlemen, Hugo. What about this nice Sam boy you got to know a little last week? You need to find some good role models for goodness sake, not sit around at home feeling sorry for yourself."

"Well—"

"I'm not finished."

Hugo nodded and grabbed at the arm of the chair, not daring to look away from his uncle as he passed up and down, along the perimeter of the rug.

"If you want to behave like a classless fool, we will treat you like one. You will not eat with us anymore. You will eat alone in the conservatory. I will be taking away your valet. You will not be out of this house after seven in the evening. Is that understood?" He stopped at last and turned to look at Hugo.

"Yes, sir."

"Good, now get out of my sight."

FOR A WEEK, the Harringtons refused to acknowledge him. They barely said a word. They kept their promise and Hugo took his meals down in the cold, airy conservatory, where the windows rattled in the wind and a cold breeze swept through.

Breakfast was simple—always the same, thick porridge. Soup or sandwich for lunch and usually stew for dinner.

Martha was always the one to bring it to him on a tray and never said a word when she did, only smiled, placed it on the edge of the table before quickly leaving him in the solitude.

Life grew very lonely in the silence of isolation, where even the servants refused to make conversation with him. He hadn't even seen Sebastian.

For the most part, Hugo kept himself confined in his room. He'd absorbed himself in books or put pencil to paper and sketched. His days were filled with nothing but birdsong and the turning of crisp pages. He gained a new appreciation for the warmth of the pale sun on his back. The trees had begun to shrivel into golds, rusts, and yellows. Autumn had begun to gradually take its hold of England and it was beautiful.

Today he had walked down as far as the Harringtons' lands stretched, through a small woodland where deer grazed and the wrinkled foliage of crooked trees cast shadows across the floor.

A river meandered through the little meadow, the sound of it trickling by in a soft song that resonated beauty and tranquillity when Hugo felt he most needed it.

By the riverbank he sat with his legs folded and a book propped open in his lap. With his chin resting in his hand, he read, quite content to enjoy the escape until the light faded from the forest and it was time to go back to Finchley Hall.

IT TOOK THREE weeks before it came—a gentle knock at his door.

Hugo opened up and made a surprised sound when it was Sebastian who waited outside, straight-faced with clasped hands. "Sir," he began at once, his eyes studying the doorframe with keen interested. He rocked on the balls of his feet, refusing to meet Hugo's eyes, which desperately sought his.

Hugo felt a stirring of guilt bubble in his stomach. He hadn't seen Sebastian to apologise to him. It'd been so long now that it seemed too late. He swallowed. "What...what can I do for you, Seb?"

"Your uncle would like you to join him for dinner this evening."

"He would?"

Sebastian nodded.

"Great! I'll be there."

"Will that be all, sir?"

Hugo bit his lip. His fingers grasped at the door frame. No. He did not want this to be all. He wanted his Sebastian back. He swallowed the flicker of pain in his chest.

"I'm sorry Sebastian," he said lightly.

Sebastian lifted his attention to meet Hugo's eyes and frowned. "You know, that would have meant more if you hadn't waited for a moment convenient for you to say that."

Hugo groaned. "I know. I...I'm not very good at this sort of thing, Sebastian. That's why I'm here, remember? I'm selfish."

"Will that be all, sir?" Sebastian asked again, dropping his gaze.

"Sure."

"Sir." Sebastian turned his back and walked away.

Eleven: The Hill

WANTING TO MAKE the most of the last weeks of pale sun, Hugo decided to take lunch and head out into the countryside, where he could enjoy the solitude and sketch. Perhaps walk into the village and attempt to get to know some of the locals. He felt like he had been exposed to the Harringtons for long enough that he could tolerate making pleasant conversation with others like them, and it would undoubtedly satisfy Uncle Henry. Especially if he brought some sensible friends around to dinner.

He had packed his pencils, sketch pad, and Mrs. Greene had prepared him a beautiful smoked ham baguette and a box of sliced fruits. Apples, grapes, oranges.

Finally, it seemed at least the servants were forgiving him. No doubt what he had said to Sebastian had been the subject of gossip since...and Hugo had tried to apologise. Perhaps that was enough to constitute a step forward, and hopefully, before long, his lunches would include a slice of cake too.

He shrugged into his mustard travelling coat, laced himself into his boots, and slipped the leather satchel over his shoulder. Hugo had intended to leave an hour ago, but without anybody around to help him organise his life, everything had taken so long.

"Hugo?" Sebastian's voice sounded quietly from behind.

Hugo straightened up and looked over his shoulder. He caught Sebastian's gaze and blinked in surprise. "Seb?"

"That bag looks heavy. May I carry it somewhere?" He had that look about him, one that said he was up to something. A look that Hugo had missed dearly.

Hugo raised a brow and smiled gently. "I...well, I'm actually going to go for a walk."

"Oh?"

"I...yes. Hm. Do you want to come?"

"Would you like me to come?"

Hugo nodded, his smile fading into a pained expression. "Please?"

Sebastian held out his arm for the bag. Hugo sighed in relief and slipped it off over his head. Grasping the strap in his hand, he hesitated. "Are you sure you want to carry it? I don't mind."

Sebastian just scoffed and pulled it from his hand. He slipped it over his shoulder and gestured towards the door. "Lead the way."

Together, they walked, still stuck in their silence, but this time, it did not feel so awkward. Hugo turned his face toward the sky and smiled, appreciating its cloudless beauty. The sun was the colour of almonds, meek and distant, but that did not make it any less bountiful.

Hugo was just glad Sebastian was by his side and not glowering at him from a distance. He knew he had to apologise again. He would, once they were far enough from Finchley Hall.

Hugo led the way, a handful of steps ahead of Sebastian, his feet following the straggling path up and up, around the outside of a hilltop. He'd never been this way before, and truly, he let his feet carry him, following his instinct.

Far too stuffy in his riding coat, he slipped it off and stuffed it beneath his arm. From the corner of his eye, he spotted Sebastian's mouth twitch into a brief smile, but the comment he knew Sebastian so desperately wanted to make never came. He held his tongue and looked away.

When they reached the peak, the view was striking.

Beneath them, the rolling moors billowed. Endless green lands stretched out beyond the horizon. Trees stood like crooked matchsticks.

A glint of silver and blue danced together along the left side of their view, scattering light. Hugo raised a hand and held it above his forehead, beaming. "Seb?"

"Yes?"

"Is that the sea close by?"

"About thirty minutes drive." He hummed, enjoying the view from over Hugo's shoulder. "You should go sometime."

Hugo turned away and nodded. He'd like that.

The spot beneath the great oak tree looked like a fine place to settle. He moved over that way and sat down. His legs folded over each other.

For a moment, Sebastian hesitated but finally sat by Hugo's side and put down his bag.

Hugo turned to smile at him and opened up his satchel. Digging a hand inside, he took out his sketch pad and pencils and set them on the ground beside them. "How've you been doing, Seb?"

Sebastian coiled his fingers around blades of grass and plucked absentmindedly at them. "Hugo, I think I'm going to leave Finchley Hall."

Hugo paused. He looked up at Sebastian who had the courage to meet his gaze, full on, no hesitation in that hard expression.

"What? Why?"

Sebastian sighed. "I think it's for the best."

"How is it for the best?" Hugo snapped.

"Hugo." Sebastian's tone remained cool, unwavering. He leaned closer, their noses inches apart. "I can't watch you destroy yourself. The drinking is bad enough, but Jesus, the drugs?" The warm pleasantness of his breath ghosted across Hugo's cheek. "And when I try to open up to you about it, you verbally harass me...after everything we've meant to each other."

Hugo made a little moan of frustration. "But you don't need to concern yourself with those things."

"Oh but, Hugo, I do. It is my concern, and I have no standing to be able to challenge you for that sort of behaviour, as you always like to remind me. I've enjoyed being your valet but, honestly, I can't stay here and get attached to you after what happened."

"Attached?"

"I really like you, Hugo."

"Oh."

Hugo snapped his head away and swallowed a mouthful of air, attempting to steady the frantic pulsing of his heart. His cheeks roared with heat. Did Sebastian really mean that? He took a moment to steady his nerves enough to say what he wanted to say.

"Seb. Don't leave because of me, really." He was overwhelmed by the feelings welling up within him. Sebastian had become the only reason he had not yet been tainted with madness in this place and now that Sebastian had admitted that he liked him...oh God.

"Waiting for you to make it up to me, after what you said has been pretty damn painful, I have to admit..." Sebastian said. "I don't want to work for somebody who can treat me with so much disrespect."

Hugo lifted his hand and covered his face, hiding his eyes from Sebastian, far too afraid, far too ashamed that he might cry. "I'm so sorry, Sebastian. Please don't leave. I really am sorry for what I said. I was so angry and upset and ashamed and I'm so sorry."

"Do you mean it?"

"Of course I do. If I stop being an asshole—hell, if I stop drinking, will you stay?" Hugo asked, daring to look at him through the gaps of his fingers.

"I don't think it's that simple. By all means, go and have fun but, goodness, know when to stop and when to take a break. I don't know if you're capable of that, but at least try to gain back control of your life."

"And you'll stay?"

Sebastian sighed. "Here's the deal. I agree to stay for now, but if I ever see you in that state again...without warning me at the very least, I'm gone. I mean it, Hugo."

Hugo nodded meekly.

"Good," he grumbled. "And, you have to make more of an effort not to be such a stuck-up brat."

Hugo nodded again.

"I have some ideas of how to deal with that part, though..."

"You do?"

A sharp tug at his hair lifted Hugo's head, and he was forced to look up at Sebastian, whose eyes darkened. He continued to pull at his hair, dragging Hugo until their lips slammed together in a rough kiss.

A tongue twirled into his mouth, and Hugo welcomed it with a moan. His mouth parted, and he brushed his lips across Sebastian's, tasting the smoky warmth of his breath.

"Climb into my lap," Sebastian hissed, low and ragged.

Hugo obliged, guided by Sebastian's hand still grasping his hair. The tightness against his scalp made him whimper, but it also made his cock twinge with anticipation.

He lifted himself off the ground and shuffled on his knees over to Sebastian who grabbed at Hugo's leg and yanked it apart from the other. Sebastian pulled him over his waist and shoved him down to sit on his thighs.

"Fuck," Hugo whispered, his face roaring with heat. A different kind of heat had begun to pool in his gut and trickle down his thighs and to his crotch.

Sebastian continued to fondle with his hair slowly, dancing across his scalp and tickling just lightly enough that he shivered.

"You see, Hugo, there are so many other ways I can have fun with you if you're feeling bored." Sebastian seized Hugo's jaw. "If you need an outlet, you only have to say." He grazed across the hollow of Hugo's throat with his teeth.

Hugo tipped his head to reveal the rolling valley of his neck, welcoming Sebastian's mouth to explore. Sebastian grazed his teeth across the skin, teasing until Hugo's flesh puckered with a spray of goose bumps.

Enjoying the sensation, Hugo closed his eyes and curled his lip upward into a pleased smile. This much craved for, much-needed attention made his heart hum. Sebastian didn't hate him for what he had said. He was on the road to being forgiven.

Hugo's mouth fell open, letting himself submit to the wet sensations that were beginning to cloud his senses.

There was a sudden sting at his neck. Hugo gasped at the spike of pain beneath his collarbone. His scrunched his shoulders and the pain subsided into an intense bliss that made his body twinge and squirm in Sebastian's lap.

Sebastian laughed. The sound ricocheted against Hugo's throat. "Hn, you're so adorable when you're like this."

Hugo glanced at Sebastian and caught him staring. That beautiful, terrible smile lit up his dark features. Hugo said nothing. His body so flushed with heat and his head so light that he didn't want to put the energy into conjuring thoughts.

It had been far too long since Sebastian had toyed with him.

"So pink and warm and...hard?" Sebastian grasped between Hugo's legs. "Oooh, yes." He squeezed across the outline of Hugo's rapidly growing erection still clothed by his trousers.

Hugo closed his eyes again. His shoulders fell, and he rolled back his head to simply lose himself in Sebastian's taunting.

There was a gentle pressure, tracing around the shape of his dick. Pleasant but not stimulating enough. Hugo gave an impatient wriggle of his hips. Sebastian continued.

"Oh come *on*. Stop teasing," Hugo hissed at last, opening his eyes to glare at his valet.

The only response from Sebastian was the removal of his hand entirely. Outraged, Hugo slammed his hips forward.

Sebastian purred. He slipped his hand beneath Hugo's shirt, where he walked his fingers across Hugo's stomach and up to his nipple. He flicked hard. Hugo gasped.

"Take off your trousers, Hugo," Sebastian said, flicking his tongue out across his earlobe.

As Hugo reached for the button, he noticed the tremor in his hands. They shook as he fumbled, trying to unfasten them. Sebastian nudged his hands away and took over.

He popped open the button and rolled down his slacks and underwear to his lower thighs. His erection popped free from the constraints of ever-tightening material and was met by a rush of cool air. The sensation made Hugo grin, satisfied that he would be getting that much-desired attention.

Sebastian grabbed hold of his dick and moaned into Hugo's ear. Hugo moaned back and thrust his hips forward.

"Please," he whispered, ashamed by his own desperate pleas.

"Since you ask so nicely," Sebastian said. He shoved Hugo's shoulder and knocked him onto his back.

Hugo tumbled onto the grass and gasped out his shock. Sebastian had never been so heavy-handed with him—so domineering and stern and honestly, Hugo's cock ached for it. He looked up at Sebastian and grazed his lips with his teeth, cheeks burning with humiliation. Hugo loved this side of Sebastian, and Sebastian knew it.

"You don't deserve this. Though, somehow, I feel like putting you back in your place. Whilst we're still sleeping together, you have to know that you don't own me. I work for you, but you answer to me. Is that understood?"

Hugo whined, the sound thick with arousal. He nodded.

Sebastian paused, still grasping between Hugo's legs, cupping his balls in his hand. He gave him a stern, chastising look. "Answer me properly. Or do you not want me to make you come?"

"S-sorry," Hugo whispered, wriggling beneath Sebastian. He felt like a mouse trapped beneath a lion's paw. "I...you, you're the one in charge. I-I understand."

Sebastian gave him a predatory smile. "Good boy." His tone dripped with honey. He pressed two fingers into Hugo's mouth, slickening them with saliva.

Knowing what was coming, Hugo pressed his feet flat against the ground and drew his legs in behind his bum, opening them wide.

Sebastian began to rub the wet fingers over the flower of Hugo's ass, tickling at it, teasing him until Hugo squirmed with need. At last, Sebastian pressed both fingers into him at once, and Hugo gasped from the sting of the shock. He reached out and grabbed at Sebastian's shirt.

Sebastian leered at Hugo as he rubbed slow spirals within him. Hugo began to relax, his body loosened beneath him, his mouth parted to let out a flurry of happy moans.

Sebastian's fingers were bliss against the tightness of his ass. Today, he was extra sensitive, and every roll of Sebastian's fingers made his hips lift from the ground. He tried to angle himself to get Sebastian's fingers deeper inside him, an action that made Sebastian laugh. He clamped down over Hugo's hips and pinned them there.

"Why so impatient, little bird?"

"Little bird?" Hugo repeated, his cheeks burning furiously. He wasn't going to admit it, but ever since the incident with Sam, Hugo hadn't even thought about touching himself. Being completely consumed by Sebastian's attention now was far too overbearing.

Despite all the teasing, Sebastian continued to thrust his fingers in and out of Hugo, loosening up the tightness of his ass. "It's apparent you haven't been stretched apart in a long time, Hugo."

"Stop it," Hugo snapped.

"Stop what?" Sebastian smiled.

"Ta-talking like that...you'll make me...c-hmm."

"So soon?" Sebastian hummed.

Hugo mewled. Sebastian was relentless. He sped his thrusts, penetrating Hugo's ass in quick, deep shoves.

His breaths came out in needy, weak pants, and he curled his toes responsively. Sebastian grabbed at the swollen mass of his testicles again, rolling the flesh between his finger and thumb. Hugo's entire groin tingled with a blissful wave of pleasure.

Sebastian gave his cock a gentle pull, and that was it.

Hugo gasped. His erection quivered, and he squirted out a spray of white semen. "Sebastian!" He gave out a strangled cry of his name and scrunched up his eyes, whimpering through the climax that made his body writhe on the grass.

He bucked his hips, and his legs twitched against the ground, tightening and releasing his muscles all at once. "Oh God!" He gave one final cry and grasped desperately for Sebastian's arms.

He pulled Sebastian down on top of him, and in response, he was showered by a rain of loving kisses.

Sebastian curled his arms around Hugo and simply held him through his post-orgasmic bliss. "I forgive you," he sighed sweetly into his ear.

Hugo nuzzled into him and squeezed at those embracing arms. "Thank you," he whispered against his chest, breathing in his scent, and at last, he felt like things would be okay again.

Twelve: The Gentleman

WHITE SMOKE FLOODED the platform. It spilled from the great steam engine's chimney and rolled over waiting passengers' feet. The bright engine gleamed—it was scarlet and black with golden detail on the chimney and wheel spokes. Its serpentine hiss was constant and a little irritating.

Hugo stood outside the first-class carriage. He lifted his pale hand to his lips and the smoke from his cigarette trailed in the air through the cloud of steam. He inhaled nicotine into his lungs; the taste was tinged with engine oil and grease.

Behind him, shoes clicked hastily across the platform. Luggage wheels rolled and shuddered over every crack in the concrete flags. Women hurried by in feathered hats, clutching their purses, and men swooped past with burlap sacks slung over their shoulders.

The controller's whistle howled its final alert, and the polished red doors were clicked shut, one by one. *Come on, Sebastian.*

Hugo pulled his brows together and flicked the butt of his cigarette onto the ground, where he crushed it beneath his shoe. Sebastian had hurried off to the bathroom the moment they'd arrived and passed their luggage over to the porter. He had been gone since.

Hugo tapped his foot on the ground and flickered his gaze between the station lounge door and the stout conductor, who was steadily worked his way along the train, securing the doors.

If they had to go back to Finchley Hall because Sebastian had made him miss their train, he was going to *murder* him.

Uncle Henry had sent Hugo on a business trip to look at some properties in London, meet with a few estate agents and narrow down the options for him. Uncle Henry wanted to buy down south. Profit was higher there. Seeing as Hugo had only just got back into Henry's good books, missing this train was the last thing he needed.

Hugo grumbled under his breath, pondering excuses to offer the grumpy conductor to make him wait. Perhaps a monetary bribe. He reached into his jacket pocket and took out his leather wallet.

A tall man veered around the corner then, dressed in a three-piece grey suit. A navy pocket square was folded into his jacket. A pretty silver pin held his matching navy tie together. He wore his sleek dark hair swept back away from his face. He walked quickly with all the elegance of a valet but with a suave smile that would not be deemed appropriate on the faces of servants at Finchley Hall.

Hugo's mouth fell open and all he could do was swallow air.

"Come on, dear chap, we'll miss the train," Sebastian said, enunciating every vowel with the utmost class. His accent was as smooth as jazz and as mischievous too. "Why on earth are you waving your wallet around like a wealthy collector in an auction house?"

He grabbed Hugo by the arm and pulled them both into the door of the first-class carriage just as the conductor arrived. He slammed it closed behind them, and a moment later, the whistle blew again.

Sebastian stood close to him in the small space between two separating doors that led into the main carriages on either side.

"Sebastian," Hugo cried, his eyes wide, his gaze flittering up and down Sebastian's very sharp attire. "Wha-what are you doing?"

"I said I was going to be here to watch you...keep you company. I can't do that effectively if I'm your valet and can't accompany you anywhere, can I?"

"B-but you can't just! *Sebastian!*" He raised his voice and stepped back, hitting the sliding door. He braced himself by grasping the handle.

"Really, Hugo, it is not good etiquette to raise your voice in public," Sebastian rumbled, his mouth lifting into a smile. His brown eyes shiny with amusement and disobedience. He laughed, turned away from Hugo at once, and disappeared through the other door and into the train carriage.

Hugo was left to stand, slouched against the opposite door, with one hand pressed to his forehead in utter astonishment. Sebastian had gone mad. Completely and utterly mad. What in heaven's name had possessed him to go rogue, steal suits, and dress up like a dandy man? Oh God. He was going to have to dismiss him.

The wailing toot of the engine blasted from the chimney, and the train began to roll forward along the tracks. The station platform slipped by the windows to reveal a spray of green fields where cattle roamed and grazed freely along the hilltops.

Hugo cursed. He had to grab Sebastian and give him the ultimatum. Cut this out and give back the suit whilst apologising profusely, or pack his bags when they got back to Finchley Hall. There were only so many things Hugo could allow Sebastian to get away with. Stealing money to pay for such a nice suit was not one of them. Hopefully they had a compartment to themselves so he could give Sebastian the grilling he deserved.

He took a step forward, nudged open the door, and paused. Instead of being greeted by rows of seating compartments, he had opened it to a room of red velvet and crystal. Dining tables of mahogany were set between brown leather chairs. A chandelier dangled, swaying gently from the ceiling with the motion of the train.

Gentleman Sebastian sat, very comfortably in a chair, a glass of bourbon already set before him on the table. He studied an open newspaper, casually perusing the articles. His legs were crossed and his foot gently tapped at the leg of the chair.

Hugo paused before him and stuffed his hands in his pockets, mulling over what to say to the man.

"Can I get you a drink, sir?" a soft-spoken man asked from the corner where he polished crystal glassware in gloved hands. The three of them were the only ones in here. Hugo shook his head and sat down opposite his rogue valet.

"Beautiful weather, don't you think, Hugo?"

"Sebastian Finch," Hugo hissed from gritted teeth.

Sebastian lifted his gaze and glanced over the top of his paper.

"You could lose your job for this nonsense."

"I know," Sebastian answered, shrugging. "I'd have certainly gone out with a bang."

"Have you lost your mind?" It was hard to sound mad whilst whispering, "Do you *want* to be fired?"

Sebastian reached out and lifted his glass of bourbon to his lips. He took a cautious sip. "No. Though, if it helps...I paid for the ticket upgrade with my savings. I didn't steal."

Hugo pinched the bridge of his nose, sitting forward in his seat. "That's *not* the point." He groaned and his eyes rolled backwards. Savings? How much in savings could a valet possibly have? He sneered at the thought. "And the suit?"

"Oh, I borrowed the suit."

"From who?"

"From you."

"It wouldn't fit you if it was my suit."

"I know, I must have accidentally ordered it in the wrong size...my mistake."

Hugo's jaw hardened, and he pressed his hands flat against the table, not knowing quite what else to do with them. He leaned forward and glared at Sebastian.

"Look, Hugo, I can switch out when we get there..." Sebastian lowered his voice into a quieter tone, wary of the crystal-polishing man over by the bar. He folded up his newspaper and put it down on the table. "I just wanted to have a little fun. I thought it would be nice not to have to hide behind doors and be in each other's company without all the formalities. Sometimes, I just want to sit and talk to you about normal things."

Hugo sat back in his seat, mulling that over. Well, that certainly eased the blow. With a grumble, he slipped his hand into his jacket pocket and fumbled around for his cigarette tin. He slipped it out, flipped open the lid, and offered one to Sebastian who shook his head.

"Does Thompson know?"

"Of course not. I was hoping to pull this off without losing my job."

"You have some nerve." Hugo snorted, locating his lighter in his pocket too. He took that out and rolled his thumb across the ignition wheel. The flame danced to life, and he drew it against his cigarette tip. He mouthed at the butt, squinted at Sebastian, and finally, laughed.

DARKNESS HAD ENVELOPED their motorcar and the stars zipped by the windows like finger-smudged paint. They rattled through London roads, headed for their quaint lodgings in Belgravia. The street lamps glowed comfortingly here.

They weren't too far now, and Hugo longed for the warmth and stillness of a good bed.

He leaned his head against Sebastian's shoulder, their fingers curled together. His eyes lolled open and closed, and Sebastian pulled him closer, easing him out of his jacket and draping it across his chest like a blanket. With that, he fell asleep.

THEIR BELGRAVIA TOWNHOUSE matched an identical row of others. Tall, pristine, white with perfectly groomed hedges and wrought-iron fences surrounding a metre of garden.

After pressing the doorbell, the two men stood waiting on the top steps. The hallway window was illuminated by a pearly yellow glow. A shadow drifted across the window, the door chain rattled, there was a metallic click, and it was pulled back.

In the hallway stood a tall man with blond hair swept into a side parting. He had friendly blue eyes and a matching smile on his thin lips, revealing the dimples in his cheeks and a ridge in his chin.

"Good evening, sirs." Plural. He elongated his vowels with the throaty roll of a French accent.

Hugo opened his mouth to reply, but Sebastian got there first. He threw out his arm and shook the valet's hand enthusiastically. "Good evening, my good man. Our cases are waiting by the foot of the steps. Do be careful. Hugo's is rather heavy. He has a knack for packing heinous amounts of belongings for relatively small trips." He guffawed and slapped Hugo enthusiastically on the back.

Hugo's face fell flat. He huffed at Sebastian, who clearly was going to milk this experience as much as possible. He caught the valet's attention, and he nodded, allowing him to continue with what he wanted to say before Sebastian's excitement got the better of him.

"My name is Raoul. I will look after you during your visit in London. Would you like to take a tea?"

"Raoul. Tea would be fantastic. I'm Mister Bentley, this here is…"

"Mister Darling."

Darling. Hugo bit at his tongue. The audacity, the insubordination. He looked up at Sebastian, cocking a brow at him. He only smirked back. Thompson would drop dead if he ever heard about this disarray. Sebastian would never work again. Goodness, he had some spine…but Hugo had to admit, he kind of admired it.

Raoul dipped into a smooth bow. "Follow me, sirs. I will show you into the drawing room where you can relax whilst I prepare your tea and carry up your cases."

The two of them followed the valet through the beautiful house. It was all very white and simplistic with little bursts of colour in the textiles. Embroidered lemon cushions, robin's egg blue curtains, red velvet chairs, and boisterous patterns on the rugs. Every ceiling was lit by an electric chandelier and the halls were filled with a light floral scent. It was small in comparison to Finchley Hall but beautifully cosy.

"Please, make yourselves comfortable. I will be back shortly," Raoul said and gestured them into the drawing room. The man turned away and the sound of creaking floorboards followed with him.

Sebastian swooped into the room and fell gracelessly into a lemon-coloured armchair beside the unlit fireplace. "Our valet is very handsome, no?" he said in a gravelly French accent. He puckered his lips and tapped his lap.

"I don't think I will ever allow myself to be attracted to another valet again."

"Oh sir, I'm hurt," Sebastian purred, patting his lap again. "Come."

For a moment, Hugo hesitated, but he could not deny that stirring urge to be close to Sebastian. There was a part of him that greatly enjoyed being undermined by the man, and Hugo knew that was a very strange, very wrong way to feel about this situation. He swallowed, but hesitantly, moved across the room and over to Sebastian.

With a dramatic sigh, he lowered himself into Sebastian's lap and wrapped his arms around his neck. In response, Sebastian's arms locked around Hugo's middle, and he dragged him closer. Secured in his embrace, Hugo felt very safe and very protected.

"I want to go to sleep," Hugo whispered. He closed his eyes and pressed his cheek to Sebastian's.

"I recommend you do. Busy day tomorrow, but not here. Raoul will be back soon."

"Oh no, the meeting isn't until the day after."

"That's not what I meant but..."

Hugo didn't reply. He had submitted to his exhaustion.

Thirteen: The Valet

THE BED WAS warm. Hugo lay on his stomach with one leg cocked and hanging over the edge. His limbs were draped in silk and the smell of vanilla, peppermint, and Sebastian Finch's shampoo.

Hugo moaned happily, filling his mouth with the fabric of his pillow. He wriggled his hips and shuffled until he nudged at a solid mass. Something stirred beside him, and a pair of arms wrapped securely around his middle.

Hugo's lids bounced apart, and he rolled his head to the right, blinking at the sight of a smirking Sebastian, who pressed his nose into Hugo's cheek and kissed him.

"I assumed you left," Hugo uttered, his voice still sleepy.

"I didn't have to. I didn't have Thompson waiting for me downstairs."

"Hmm, aren't worried about Raoul?"

"He won't come until you call for him," Sebastian said, kissing the spot beneath his ear.

"This is nice. Let's not call for him yet."

Sebastian nodded his agreement and closed his lips around Hugo's. The two of them melted into a soft, slow kiss. Their lips attentively rolled together, and Sebastian lost his fingers in Hugo's hair.

Hugo moaned, pleased at the careful caressing of their mouths. It wasn't so often that Sebastian kissed him with such care, such warmth. They were usually all desperate and brazen. Today, Sebastian had time and freedom, and he was going to use it as best as he could. Already, Hugo was longing for the next time they would be able to do this again.

A tug at his hair angled back his head to expose the line of his throat. Hugo closed his eyes and moaned out his anticipation.

Sebastian grunted, his breath blowing out across his throat. He bit down and rolled Hugo's skin between his teeth. Lapping out his tongue, he licked and sucked at the flesh.

Hugo cried out.

Sebastian stopped then and removed his mouth from Hugo's throat. "Your neck is so wonderfully sensitive."

"It is." Hugo hummed happily.

"Let's not get too excited just yet."

"Why not?"

"Because, I want to have some fun with you first."

"Oh no." Hugo wriggled back, creating more space between their hips.

Sebastian's smile was near menacing. He lifted himself up and propped his elbow on the pillow, those doe eyes locked with Hugo's. "Why don't you get me dressed?"

Hugo's brow creased in confusion. "Pardon?"

"You heard me."

"I did but..."

"Get me dressed, and I'll give you an orgasm," Sebastian growled and slapped him firmly across the ass.

Hugo squeaked, scrambled upwards, and clambered out of bed. He rubbed at his behind, his cheeks flourished red. "Okay, fine."

"Fine, what?"

"Fine, I'll get you dressed."

"Fine, *sir*. Don't forget your place when you talk to me, valet Hugo."

"Don't push your luck, Finch."

Sebastian grinned, his eyes gleaming, but he pressed his lips together and said nothing more.

Hugo crossed the room and opened the wardrobe where Raoul had hung the clothes. He paused then and looked over his shoulder towards Sebastian. "You have more suits?"

"No, I'll just have to wear what I wore yesterday."

"Oh, Sebastian, that won't do. Raoul will notice."

"I suppose..."

"Looks like I'll have to take you shopping."

"You can't do that," Sebastian grumbled and wriggled higher up the bed. He leaned into the cushioned headboard and frowned at such a suggestion.

"Oh I can. If we're going to play this game, we have to play it properly. Wear one of my shirts, just roll up the sleeves. My slacks will be short on you, so wear yesterday's and we'll get you some new things in town."

"Sir, honestly—"

"I insist."

"Well, as long as the colour schemes you insist upon aren't as vulgar as your own."

Hugo rolled his eyes and elected to ignore Sebastian.

Sebastian swung his legs over the bed and perched himself on the edge, his bare feet tracing circles across the floor.

Hugo approached him with a crisp white shirt, and Sebastian lifted his arms for him. With some reluctance, Hugo began.

Sebastian watched with keen interest as Hugo worked his hands along the shirt, fastening the buttons through the wrong holes at first. Hugo grumbled at the lopsided mess and popped his shirt open again.

"This is harder when it's somebody else." Hugo sighed, his lip twitching into a frown.

"Take your time," Sebastian said and reached out to ruffle Hugo's hair affectionately.

Hugo touched the roof of his mouth with his tongue whilst he concentrated. He lined the shirt properly and refastened Sebastian into it.

"I don't know how you do this so quickly." Hugo snorted and sat back on his heels to admire his handiwork.

"Practice makes perfect, I suppose."

Hugo nodded as he slipped a silk tie around Sebastian's neck—a nice matte silvery colour with navy pinhead dots across it. He crossed the tie over and looped the lengths together, creating an elegant knot at his throat.

Hugo pulled it tighter at the top of his collar and smiled. "The tie suits you."

"It's a tad eccentric." Sebastian pouted, lifting the material. "I'd have preferred something plain."

"It is not eccentric. Besides, I don't own plain, you damn bluenose," Hugo scoffed.

Next came the slacks—easy. Sebastian stood from the edge of the bed and gracefully stepped into them. Hugo dropped down onto his knees to fasten him in. He looked up at Sebastian from where he knelt before him and grinned. He was done.

"I didn't think you'd be able to tie the tie..."

"Oh, come off it. Every respectable gentleman knows how to tie a simple tie. I can dress myself, you know." He'd had to do it for the month he'd not had a valet around.

Hugo stood and reached his arms above his head, wriggling his fingers as he stretched. "Okay. Now my turn."

"Not just yet. Make the bed," Sebastian said and gestured to the rumpled duvet. He neatened the hem of his shirt and retucked it into his trousers, looking at Hugo, waiting for his reaction.

"Don't be so absurd. Raoul can do that when he gets in."

"Why don't you play along, Hugo?" Sebastian said coldly. His tone had taken on that deep gravelly ruggedness he usually reserved for grunting into Hugo's ear whilst pounding into him.

A heat radiated through him at once. His gaze met Sebastian's hard determined eyes, and he swallowed, then lowered his eyes and turned his attention to the duvet instead. His cheeks were already hot. It was an instant reaction to Sebastian whenever he took on *that* tone. How ridiculous.

Hugo sighed but nodded and stepped over to the bed. Sebastian was lucky he was handsome enough that Hugo was willing to play along with these stupid games, no matter how ridiculous they were. If it got him that much sought-after attention from Sebastian, he would always play along. Hugo knew he was willing to do almost anything for it.

Hugo grabbed the corners of the duvet and began to shake it out. He flicked it up, and it fanned into the air and unravelled itself, then fell slowly, back into place, straighter. Hugo leaned down over the bed to smooth out the creases into perfection, and suddenly, he realised Sebastian's intentions in making him do this.

For a moment, Hugo paused. He could feel Sebastian's gaze on him as he stood behind, drinking in the sight of Hugo, naked and bending over the bed to fix it. Hugo stuck his ass into the air to give Sebastian a view he could appreciate just a little more.

He edged around the bed, pulling the material out as he moved, and when he stopped, he parted his legs. The bed was perfection, but Hugo didn't want to be done. His hand glided across the surface of the silk, appreciating the slippery softness beneath his fingers.

Sebastian dropped his hands onto Hugo's cheeks and pinched hard. "You're beautiful, Hugo."

Hugo smiled and pushed his hips back, pressing his ass against those hands. Thumbs rolled across the flesh and fingers began to knead and play with the muscles, rubbing hard, circular motions against him.

Hugo closed his eyes and mewled happily at the soothing sensation.

Sebastian paused his movement. "Next, you have to dust," he said matter-of-factly.

Hugo's face fell. All traces of bliss lost. Nope. This was a step too far. No way was he going to reduce himself to *dusting*. Next, Sebastian would have him on his knees and scrubbing the toilet bowl. Absolutely not!

"You are un-bel-ieveable Sebastian Finch," He snapped his head around to look back at the man, displeasure written all over his face.

His look was met with a severe expression from Sebastian. Hugo looked down, and the man's pyjama bottoms were unfastened and rolled down to beneath his bum along with his underwear. His erect cock stood tall.

All the sarcastic, snappy words that had begun to wheel in Hugo's head fizzled out immediately. He blinked his shock and looked away, heat pooling down to his cock.

"Very good, *sir*," Hugo answered instead. The words made his stomach flutter. Submitting to Sebastian's game stirred something up within him. It made his cock respond eagerly. His cheeks burned with shame. He liked this.

Sebastian moved from behind him, but Hugo didn't feel as if he ought to move. He stayed put with his arms stretched out in front of him. The sound of Sebastian's footsteps echoed as he walked across the room, and Hugo shivered, waiting anxiously for him to return. The door creaked open, Sebastian left, and Hugo felt suffocated by the silence that followed.

Left to concentrate on the thrumming beat of his heart. It flurried about his chest. Quick, anxious, loud, it rattled over his bones.

He closed his eyes and smiled against the silence, searching for beauty within its tranquillity, appreciating the moment for what it was. Here, away from the formalities of Finchley Hall. A day of peace with no tasks to attend to, but for the trivial ones Sebastian decided to set. No dinners to show face for. A day where he did not need to be a gentleman for other people's eyes, but he could be raw and himself entirely, guided by Sebastian Finch and his wicked mind.

Footsteps again. Hugo peeked one eye open and looked ahead at the wall. The steps grew louder and the door squeaked. The floorboards creaked as Sebastian crept closer, and then, something sleek and soft stroked across the curve of his ass.

Hugo groaned at the tickling of something as it swept across his bottom. He bit his lip but could not withhold the giggle. It spluttered free, and he laughed out loud at the taunting sensation sweeping from side to side.

"Dust," Sebastian hummed. The teasing stopped, and something smooth and hard was slipped into his hand. The handle of a feather duster.

Hugo sighed but nodded his head, and with that, he pushed himself away from the bed and straightened up. He flickered his hand, waving the duster from side to side as if to test it out. His gaze whisked about the room, searching out something he could use it on.

Sebastian settled himself on the bed. Crossing his legs, he sat back and followed Hugo about the room with his eyes.

Hugo wasn't quite sure what to do with it—he couldn't gauge how to brandish his duster in a way that would be deemed sexy. He waved it across the surface of the bookshelf and the top of the dresser as he walked. The feathers slipped over the edging of the mirror frame, and then he moved back along the bed to tickle at Sebastian's neck as he passed.

Sebastian smiled encouragingly. "Don't forget the skirting boards."

Hugo paused by the wall and bent down, lowering his arm to stroke the feathers across the wooden ledge. He worked the duster from left to right, bending lower and pushing out his ass. He began to sway his hips from side to side, following the motion of his cleaning tool. This brought some very pleased noises from Sebastian.

"I can't do this anymore," Sebastian said and flung himself off the bed. He closed the distance between the two of them and snatched Hugo by his waist. He grabbed the duster from his hand and shoved Hugo forward.

Hugo squeaked out his surprise and turned to rest his cheek on the cool wall. "I thought you had more willpower than that, old man."

"Old man?" Sebastian retorted, affronted. "I'm twenty-four!" He grabbed a fistful of Hugo's hair and pulled it, yanking back his head. Hugo moaned at the rough handling.

The duster disappeared between Hugo's warm thighs, and the feathers teased. A gentle, tantalising sensation that made his hair stand on end and his already solid cock twinge with excitement.

Sebastian swept the silky material up and down between his legs and Hugo's breath hitched. He pressed his palms flat against the wall. The fibres ghosted along the underside of his testicles and Hugo's head rolled back in joy. He never thought he would enjoy being humiliated so much.

"Stand with your legs further apart," Sebastian demanded quietly, the feathers still pressing against his balls.

Hugo lifted a leg and stretched it out, placing it down further away from the other. The moment his bare foot touched, a cold slippery finger pressed into him. Hugo gasped. The sound faded into a heated moan as Sebastian rubbed a circular motion inside the walls of his entrance.

At once, he relaxed and his shoulders dropped, the tension easing out of him. Not once had he felt uncomfortable with any part of Sebastian inside him. Only pleasure or overwhelming bliss.

"Thank you." He panted with exasperated desperation.

"Thank you, what?"

Hugo whined. "Thank you, sir."

"Good boy," Sebastian said, and Hugo could hear the smile of victory in his voice.

Sebastian pressed a second finger inside him, and Hugo's ass stretched apart with Sebastian's careful scissoring motions. He took his time with Hugo, rubbing those fingers deeper into his ass with each gentle thrust.

Sebastian rested his other hand on the small of Hugo's back, pressing hard whenever Hugo tried to wriggle. Gradually, the tightness of his muscles was massaged out of him, until he was loose and slack against the wall.

When Sebastian removed his fingers, Hugo's face tightened in protest, but he held out, for he knew what would follow.

The squelching sound of lubricant being lacquered across a surface came from behind Hugo. He cocked his head and waited, his toes curling eagerly. "Please, sir," he said urgently.

Sebastian dropped his hand onto his hip. The tip of something hard and smooth began to press into Hugo. Something that did not have the sheer fullness of Sebastian's cock. It was slender and long as it ploughed up and into Hugo.

"Wh-what's that?" he asked, panicked.

"You get one guess. If you guess wrong, I'll stop." Sebastian chuckled, twisting the object further into him.

"Please." Hugo still moaned with delight at being filled by *something*.

"That's not your guess, is it?" Sebastian laughed.

Hugo shook his head.

"So?"

"I-is it...the duster?" he whispered, lowering his hips toward the wall to press his cock against the cool surface.

"Of course," Sebastian mused. Thrusting harder into Hugo.

Hugo moaned loud and flushed at the beautiful sensation rubbing at his insides. "F-fuck."

He lifted his cheek away from the wall and leaned his forehead against the surface instead. He closed his eyes and allowed his hips to be rocked forward. The length of his cock glided across the surface of the wall with every steady motion. "I-I want your dick inside me," he breathed out, his voice warbling.

A sudden sharp sting whipped across his left ass cheek. Fast and hot, it left a warmth radiating across the mark Sebastian had surely left behind. Hugo hissed, the sound turning into an aroused grunt of approval at that sharp slap.

"Wh-what was that for?" he squeaked, so very pleased. His face touched the wall so he didn't have to face Sebastian with this amount of arousal fixed across his face.

"I already warned you. You're in no position to give orders," Sebastian growled, heavy and hot into his ear. All the same, the length of the handle was pulled from inside him and clattered on the table behind. "Besides..." Sebastian began. Seizing a fistful of his hair, he urged Hugo's head around to look his way. "You haven't done a single thing for me. It's all been about you until now. You're going to have to work for it." With that, he dragged Hugo's head down and guided him between Sebastian's legs.

Hugo faltered and fell, letting his head disappear between Sebastian's thighs. Rather than running his tongue along his dick, Hugo flicked it out and trailed it along the line of his asshole and swirled it around the opening. This earned him a shocked gasp from Sebastian. Sebastian's legs quivered around him, tightening briefly around his head, before Sebastian forced them back apart.

Hugo smiled, pleased with himself, and pressed his tongue into the folds of his entrance. His tongue convulsed as he forced it deep into Sebastian's ass, letting it shiver and quake against the walls of his inner core.

Hugo made sure to use plenty of saliva as he built up a quick pace, flicking his tongue into Sebastian. He propelled it in and out of him, pressing deeper and deeper each time, until his nose was buried against the line of his cheeks.

Sebastian's moans were beautiful. Relentless and full bodied, they fell from his mouth until Hugo was drunk on them.

Sebastian tightened his hand in Hugo's hair, moans growing in volume. He shivered against Hugo.

At once, Sebastian dragged him away, shaking his head furiously. "God...God no, I-I'll come if you don't stop," he said, breathless. He released his grip on Hugo's hair and sat back a little, patting at his lap. "Come, ride me."

Satisfied, Hugo nodded and waited for Sebastian to settle himself at the edge of the bed, his feet resting on the bedroom floor.

Hugo crawled over to him and moved to straddle his lap. He squirmed and leaned down to kiss along the line of his throat. "You sound beautiful when you moan." He chuckled, the laugh soon silenced by the firm grope of hands at his ass.

Sebastian gripped onto his hips and pulled Hugo down, over the top of his erection. The tip was slick and slippery with lubricant. Hugo sighed in pleasant surprise.

"W-when did you?"

"Stop talking," Sebastian growled and knocked his hips upwards. The length of him pushed into the ring of tight muscles, and Hugo slipped down the entirety of his cock.

"Oh God," Hugo moaned, overwhelmed by the sensation of being so suddenly filled by the whole of Sebastian's cock in one swooping motion. He settled down against him, allowing himself a moment to adjust. "So big." He buried his face into the crook of Sebastian's neck.

Sebastian grabbed his thighs then and began to bounce him along the pole of his dick. Hugo worked with him, bouncing up and down, already so very aroused, it didn't take long until he was rolling his head back and moaning in glee.

The sound of their skin smacking together drove Hugo wild with lust. He closed his eyes and his cheeks roared with heat. That tantalising friction that rubbed within him—slick, hot, and quick—tipped him over the edge. Without meaning to, he came. A spray of semen squirted from the tip of his cock, and he was left gasping out strangled moans of delight. His toes curled as an orgasm rocked through him. He cried out, loud and giddy, and tightened his fingers on Sebastian's shoulders.

Then he was done. He slumped, exhausted, against Sebastian's chest and his efforts were rewarded by a shower of sweet kisses.

Sebastian purred into his ear and gently, gently eased out of him. He urged Hugo to lie on his back. Once he did, Sebastian straddled him. "Look at me," he hissed, his eyes dark with lust. Sebastian's slick cock was still rock hard.

Sebastian began to stroke himself. His hand slipped up and down, pulling at his erection with quick, needy tugs. His eyes met Hugo's, who gazed up as his valet's face twisted with pure bliss.

As he stroked himself, Sebastian's stare burned into his, dark and gleaming. His lips parted, a stray, damp lock dangled before his eyes, and at last he came. A beautiful moan left him as his sticky seed squirted out along the curve of Hugo's neck.

Sebastian collapsed down beside Hugo and pulled him in close, possessively against his body. Together they lay, limbs entwined, and it took no time before Hugo succumbed to the welcoming arms of sleep.

Fourteen: Autumn Rain

AMONGST THE GLITZ of Piccadilly Circus, where engines growled as black cabs whipped past and horns pipped in a chaos of sound, Hugo and Sebastian waded their way through the crowd.

Sebastian was all wide-eyed and open-mouthed. He took in the sheer immenseness of the West End. Surely, he'd never seen so many cars in his life. Here they came, one after the other, circling the glorious fountain in which Eros balanced on one foot. His bronze wings pointed toward the sky and his bow angled at the passing crowd, who were too busy to notice him.

Holding the top of his panama, Sebastian tipped back his head. He gazed in awe at the advertisement boards with their stark bold letters. They hung from every building, cluttered every available wall. Bold lights brimmed the entrances of theatres and cinemas, all nestled snugly together along Shaftesbury Avenue.

Hugo smiled. Seeing Sebastian's beautiful eyes alight with such wonder as he took in the hustle and bustle of the capital made a warmth ripple through his chest and spread deep into his core.

He took a hold of Sebastian's upper arm and gently pulled at him. "Come on. We'll be late."

"Where are we even going?" Sebastian asked, still scanning the storefronts, but at least now, he was walking with a little more haste.

"The opera."

"You don't sound thrilled."

"God no, I hate the opera," Hugo said as they made their way through the explosion of people.

Sebastian tipped his head, looking down at Hugo, and cocked a brow. "Not the best choice of activity then, sir," he mused. "Then why did you buy the tickets?" His expression faltered and he stopped abruptly. "Wait, Hugo..."

Hugo glowered and nudged him with his elbow. "We're in the way."

Erratic Londoners grumbled as they looped around the obstacle of the two men. A heavy bag knocked against Hugo's legs, and he shuffled closer to Sebastian, grabbed him by the arm, and urged him to continue walking. The two of them started again.

"Hugo, really, you didn't have to. I'm flattered."

Hugo rolled his eyes and looked back at Sebastian who followed very closely behind him. "Just say thank you. Don't be so humble."

Sebastian grinned. "Thank you."

Hugo nodded. "You're welcome." Then he turned away. It was a good idea to watch where you were going in places like this. The rush of it all was thrilling. People zigzagging, hurrying, even though they had no place to be. The lights, the smells, the sounds. For the first time, Hugo felt like he was home.

"Almost seems like a sort of date," Sebastian said quite suddenly.

"It is a date," Hugo answered, not looking back at him.

"Didn't think you could ever be quite so sweet."

"Watch it."

Sebastian snorted. "I'm terrified."

Hugo led them into the exquisite beauty of the opera house, all lined in red velvet. Intricately upholstered chairs, embroidered with complex floral designs in gold. Mahogany and gold banisters carved with the faces of chubby cherubs, ivy leaves, and their tendrils.

They were handed glasses of champagne upon arrival and escorted to their box. Glossy programmes were slipped into their hands, and they were left to get comfy amongst the excited ambiance of the preshow buzz.

"The opera is, of course, in Italian. The second booklet has the translations inside."

Sebastian looked down at the booklet and smiled. "I don't need them."

"Why not?"

"I speak Italian."

"What do you mean, you speak Italian?" Hugo grunted and sat forward to fix Sebastian a look.

"My mama is Italian," Sebastian said, putting the booklet down against the balcony.

"What? You kept that quiet."

"Ah, it never came up."

Hugo's lip curled into an annoyed grimace.

Sebastian flickered a glance back at Hugo, and his eyes crinkled at the corners. Hugo knew that look. He wanted to say something cocky, but he was holding it back.

Hugo folded his arm. "What else don't I know about you?"

"Most things, I'd say."

"Well, my dear Sebastian, we have a lot of talking to do."

His heart seemed to shrivel in his chest. It slipped down and fell into his stomach. Was that guilt? Perhaps. Sebastian knew everything about him, and Hugo hadn't bothered, even once, to ask about Sebastian's life. About his parents, his childhood, his dreams, his aspirations. What did he do when he wasn't serving Hugo? Did he paint? Did he play cricket? He didn't have a clue. Hugo pinched his nose. He was such an *asshole*.

The house lights went down, casting the theatre into darkness, and the rumbling of voices stilled into silence. The orchestra thrummed to life, and the red curtains drew apart to reveal the grotty set of an apartment interior and a shivering painter and poet. Hugo leaned forward and propped his elbows on the frame of the balcony. Thirty minutes in, he was asleep.

When he woke, it was to a gentle friction brushing along his thigh. Wandering fingers massaged along his leg. A pleasant sensation that made a flurry of goose bumps pucker across his arms.

Hugo made a confused noise in his throat and lifted his head from the balcony ledge. With cheeks flushed and eyes foggy with sleep, he glanced at Sebastian and frowned.

"Ass," he huffed, sitting back. "I was sleeping well."

"If you're bored, I can make things a little more interesting for you...if you like?" Sebastian squeezed hard at his thigh and then stopped, waiting for a response from Hugo.

Hugo blinked at him in a daze but nodded.

Sebastian slipped his hand to his inner thigh. "May I?"

Hugo attempted to focus. He looked back at Sebastian's face. He looked beautiful with his soft lips parted. He leaned against Hugo to whisper into his ear, so close Hugo could almost taste the warmth of his breath.

"Can I play with your cock?"

Hugo's cheeks burned, but he nodded again. "Yes," he whispered back and pushed his legs apart, encouraging Sebastian.

Sebastian made a happy sound in his throat and bit at Hugo's ear. He slipped his hand down the front of Hugo's trousers and it disappeared into his boxers. Sebastian curled cool fingers around his flaccid cock and began to stroke it delicately. The cold touch made Hugo shiver, and he bit at his lip to stop the gasp, drawing in a deep breath instead.

Sebastian's attention trailed away from Hugo, though, and he looked back to the stage, where the leading lady frantically warbled. The vibrato was fleeting. It was a power that resonated in Hugo's chest, shaking him to the core, and he couldn't tell if the goose bumps were from the music or from the hand job.

Those hands were beautiful. Massaging along his cock, starting at the base, he worked his fingers up, rubbing them in circles over his slowly hardening length. A second hand joined the first, and Sebastian slipped his fingers beneath his balls, rolling them between his finger and thumb. He played with them enthusiastically, and all the while, his eyes remained glued to the stage.

Hugo watched him with a lopsided glare. The bastard wasn't even slightly fazed by what he was doing, in a public theatre. How the hell was he going to sit and watch the opera now whilst carrying out his perversions on Hugo at the same time?

Sebastian tugged at his cock.

"Oh God," Hugo whimpered at last and his glare faltered into an expression of pure arousal.

Sebastian smirked.

"Sebastian," Hugo whined. "Somebody w-will see."

"No, they won't. Close your eyes," he whispered in his ear.

Hugo did. The opera house was shrouded in darkness and all that remained was the calling bird on stage and those sweet, teasing sensations across his cock.

Hugo moaned out his delight and his head rolled backwards to rest on his seat. Sebastian grasped firmly at the base of him. He moaned out, hot breath against his neck. There was a hand in his hair and it grasped tight.

"W-what?" Hugo's voice was drowned out under the operatic screaming.

Sebastian bit hard at his ear.

Hugo gasped. His eyes flew open. He looked over to a very stoic Sebastian.

"I thought I told you to close your eyes?"

Hugo snapped them shut again. His heart shuddered. That stern tone Sebastian took with him went straight to his cock.

Sebastian continued working his hand along the length of his dick. With his eyes closed and his head clouded by sleep, he was extra sensitive today. Every brush and stroke across his cock created a rippling wave of pleasure that shuddered through him and made his legs tremble with need. The sensation rolled from the base to the tip, fingers traced in circular patterns, brushed across his tip, massaged his testicles until he was weeping precum.

There was a sting at his lip where Sebastian bit down against his mouth. He grasped the base of him. Those teasing, tentative strokes stopped. Instead, he began quick-paced pumps along the length of his cock, rolling his hand along him with fervour.

Hugo panted at the change in pace and opened his mouth to groan out elated, happy moans. At once, Sebastian covered his mouth with a hand and clamped down tight. It was a good job too, for the sounds that followed were relentless screams of joy as an orgasm rolled over him, all drowned out against Sebastian's silencing hand.

His thighs went rigid; his buttocks clenched tight. His legs slapped together as he came across Sebastian's hand. A slippery, warm trail of fluid that dripped down between the gaps of Sebastian's fingers.

Sebastian's stroking slowed into gentle, soft brushes until Hugo stopped squirming in his seat.

Once he had milked him of every drop, he leaned over Hugo and pressed a kiss to his temple. "You're beautiful."

Hugo slumped back in his chair, breathless and flushed, his eyes lit with bliss. Sebastian reached into his pocket, produced a navy handkerchief, and proceeded to wipe himself clean with it.

"That's your favourite colour," Hugo mused, drunk on his orgasm. He fumbled with the button of his trousers.

Sebastian frowned. "White..." he said, frowning at the come over the back of his hand, "or blue?"

"Navy." Hugo scoffed.

Sebastian laughed. "It is. I think we should go. It's about to end soon anyway."

Giggling like naughty school children, Sebastian and Hugo stumbled through the doors of the opera house, much to the ushers' dismay. Leaving the theatre early was a disgusting act of rebellion.

Outside, the streets were awash with rain. Puddles of water reflected ghosts of light, ethereal and warm. The buildings were a blur of orange and grey.

It was considerably less busy now. Nobody wanted to be caught in the rain that bounced along the streets like scattered marbles. It fell heavy and hard.

Hugo paused beneath the theatre balcony, looking ahead at the gloom. "Good God, we didn't even bring an umbrella."

Sebastian laughed at Hugo's horror. "It's only a little bit of rain, Hugo." He took Hugo's arm and pulled him along. They stepped out from beneath their shelter and into the rain.

It rattled against the rim of Hugo's hat, thumped against his shoulders. It dripped beneath the collar of his shirt, and a single droplet rolled down the line of his spine.

Hugo shuddered, disgusted. "This is terrible. Let's get a cab, quick."

Sebastian chuckled and pulled Hugo by the arm through the washed-out streets. "This is what we get for daring to leave the opera early!"

Together, they hurried along the pavement, Sebastian leading the way. Hugo's socks were soggy inside his brogues, and he groaned at the sensation of wool clinging to his feet as he walked. His feet squelched with every step until they finally managed to flag down a cab.

They clambered into the back and huddled together, shivering all the way back to Belgravia.

There was something rather therapeutic about rain when you weren't stuck out in it. The way it bounced with a melodic rhythm against the glass. The gentle hiss of it whizzing by. Its soft sigh as it trickled along the gutters. It was beautiful and brought with it the temptation of sleep and the desire for warmth, to be curled up beneath a feather-filled duvet and dream. So badly, he wanted to burrow into Sebastian.

Hugo was grateful when they arrived outside their townhouse and left Sebastian to pay their driver as he hopped out of the car and darted up the steps.

When he stepped inside, Hugo was enveloped by a warmth that instantly soothed him. He sighed out his relief and hung up his soaked hat on the rack. His clothes clung to him, heavy and sodden with water. He couldn't wait to peel them off and wrap up.

"So. Cold," he huffed, limbs trembling.

"Well, it'll be my pleasure to warm you up." Sebastian hummed as he stepped through the door, hanging up his own hat beside Hugo's.

The sound of footsteps coming up the stairs averted Hugo's attention, and sure enough, the smiling blond appeared at the top of the staircase, armed with a bundle of towels.

"Oh, you are good," Hugo said as Raoul approached and handed over the towel.

"So thoughtful too," Sebastian added, working his fingers along the buttons of his coat.

Raoul, bashful as he was, bit his lip and turned his gaze to the floor. He lifted the second towel and offered it to Sebastian who took it quickly.

"How very efficient you are in a time of need," he said, throwing the towel around his shoulders and hanging up his drenched coat.

Raoul clasped his hands together and lowered his head. "Will that be all, sirs?"

Hugo tipped his head, unsure.

"I can take it from here, Raoul, get an early night," Sebastian suggested.

Raoul dipped into a smooth, grateful bow.

Hugo grinned. "Goodnight, Raoul."

"Bonne nuit." Raoul said, looking up at them both with a smile setting on his lips before he disappeared back downstairs.

Together, Hugo and Sebastian climbed the staircase to retire to their rooms for the night.

Once inside, Sebastian's hands fell onto the towel draped across Hugo's head and began to scrub, heavy-handed at his hair.

"Sebastian." Hugo scoffed, hunching up his shoulders and shying away from his hands.

"Just a moment. You can't go to bed with wet hair," Sebastian cooed, slowing down a little. He removed the towel from Hugo's head and began to comb his fingers through the damp straggles of blond hair, combing it back from his face. "There, that's better. Can't have you catching a death of cold on my watch."

The rain continued outside, drizzling against the window and washing over the view of the garden with grey. Sebastian swept over and pulled the curtains together to blot out the misery. The rhythmic pitter-patter of raindrops as they bounced over the glass was beautifully therapeutic.

Raoul had lit the fire. Embers glowed ruby and a calming warmth crept through the room. Orange flames danced on the firewood and cast flickering shadows that stretched out across the floorboards.

"Allow me to play valet again," Sebastian said quite suddenly as he pulled his clinging shirt off over his head and tossed it into the wash basket.

"To *play* valet," Hugo responded flatly.

Sebastian only smiled and stepped closer. He reached out and began to unfasten Hugo's shirt buttons. "I guess I should get used to knowing my place again, sir."

"Oh, Sebastian, you've never known your place. You're nothing but a rebel."

"Touché..."

The damp fabric of Hugo's shirt was pulled away to reveal the pink flush of his skin. Sebastian kissed him over the top of his heart. His lips were warm and soft and reassuring. The heat of them whispered upward, to colour his cheeks.

"Be gentle with me," Hugo whispered.

"Oh, I intend to be." Sebastian's voice, a gentle lull, willed Hugo's eyes to close. He brushed the ghost of his fingers along the line of Hugo's jaw and cupped his chin in his grasp, then turned Hugo's face toward him and kissed him, slow and deep. Hugo moaned at the taste of him. He parted his lips, welcoming the familiar warmth of that tongue into his mouth.

Sebastian plucked open the button of his slacks and pulled them down from his hips. They landed in a pool at his ankles, and Sebastian broke their kiss with a happy little hum.

"You're very cute," Sebastian mused.

"I know."

Sebastian laughed and wrapped the cotton towel snugly around Hugo's frame. He rubbed his hands along his towelled arms, attempting to force some warmth back into him.

"Hmm, get into bed, sir. You're practically frozen." He pressed his hand against his shoulders, spun him around, and nudged him in that direction.

Hugo obliged, quite happy to lie down. He burrowed himself beneath the covers until only his head poked out. "Join me."

"I will, I will, just...let me get dry first."

Hugo followed Sebastian with his eyes as he wriggled out of his trousers. A brief smile flickered across Hugo's face when he caught a flash of his cock. "Hmm, you could put more effort into some form of striptease for me." He chuckled.

"I'm far too cold that sort of debauchery." Sebastian scoffed and abruptly ended the fun by wrapping himself up in a bathrobe.

Hugo's face fell and he pouted like a petulant child. "Such a spoilsport."

"You're acting like you've never seen my cock." Sebastian snickered as he crossed back over to the foot of the bed.

He fell dramatically onto the mattress, crawled up the bed, and shimmied his way beneath the covers, joining Hugo.

The thunder boomed then with a ferocity that made the windows rattle. It caused Sebastian to flinch. His dark eyes grew wide and he tightened his grip on the duvet cover.

"You're scared of thunder?" Hugo asked.

Sebastian puffed out his cheeks. "It makes me tense. Reminds me of the trenches."

"Oh." Hugo grabbed Sebastian by the waist and pulled him closer. He offered him a sympathetic smile and reached out to tuck a stray lock of Sebastian's hair behind his ear. "Do you want to talk about it?"

Sebastian closed his eyes and shook his head. The next crack of thunder made him gasp and he pressed closer against Hugo's chest. "Hmm, no, I'd rather tell you about how much trouble I used to get into at school."

Hugo laughed. "That doesn't surprise me one bit."

They lay together in each other's arms. The roaring thunder mellowed, and slowly, the tension melted from Sebastian's shoulders. Hugo tried to distract him by talking about their lives—their childhoods, their biggest fears, their dreams, their disappointments, about each other, until the sun began to creep back into the sky.

As PAINFUL AS it was to see those beautiful days together come to an end, they did. Surviving on little sleep, Sebastian and Hugo woke for the last time, curled into each other in bed.

Hugo had gotten through his meetings and spent those moments in between lazing around with Sebastian. He had never felt so content with life here. Never felt so much attachment to another human being before. So, it was with a heavy heart that they bid Raoul farewell with promises to visit London again soon and left to return to life at Finchley Hall.

Fifteen: Copper & Lead

THAT DAY, THE sky had forgotten to be blue. Fine rain shivered from the murky mist. It hung from the scarce tree branches and clung to the grasses like scattered pearls. The countryside had faded into darker hues. Soon the whispering winter would creep in and cover the hills in white with her icy breath.

Wrinkled leaves scattered the roadside as they rumbled over the moors. The sound of rain pitter-pattered against the windscreen and hissed beneath the tyres as they rolled through puddles.

Sebastian sat beside Hugo with an easy smile about his mouth, his hands clasped together and resting in his lap. Now dressed again in his valet blacks, his hair swept back into its orderly sleekness. Returning to reality did not seem to dampen Sebastian's spirits as it did Hugo's.

He smiled weakly at Sebastian, who gazed idly out of the window, watching the soggy countryside scenery. Perhaps returning to Finchley Hall would not be so bad if Sebastian was around to keep him company.

A modest life in a quaint London townhouse had opened his eyes. It was Sebastian who remained the most important factor in surviving his life of sensibilities.

Hugo sighed. They were getting close now. They'd passed that familiar mossy stone bridge that led across the river. They had about half a mile ahead of them.

He plucked his cigarette tin from his pocket and flipped open the lid. Taking one out, he pressed it into his mouth and felt around for his lighter. He patted across his jacket pockets and felt the inside his slacks to no avail.

"Sebastian?"

He turned. "Yes, sir?"

"I don't seem to be able to find my light…"

"I put it in your inner left pocket, sir."

Hugo dipped his hand inside. "Aaah, quite." He took it from there.

Hugo sparked up and lit the cigarette. Sebastian turned away.

They rolled down their final dip in the hill and there, resting at the foot of it, were the lands of Finchley Hall.

"I do hope luncheon is served immediately when we arrive back," Hugo grunted, puffing at the end of his cigarette.

"It's not like Mrs. Greene to be slack on timings, sir. So, I imagine it will be," Sebastian answered, gaze fluttering to his timepiece before tucking it away.

The gates were open, and they slowed as they meandered around the fountain and then stopped before those ornate steps that curled up to the door.

Sebastian was quick to scramble from the car.

Charles clambered from the driver's seat and stepped around to open up Hugo's door, leaving Sebastian to take care of the bags.

"Good trip, sir?" Charles asked, offering Hugo a bit of a smile.

"Absolutely brilliant, Charles. Just perfect," Hugo answered easily, grabbing his hat from the seat as he stepped out of the back. He dropped it onto his head and heaved out a sigh. Already, he missed the playfulness of gentleman Sebastian.

He curled his finger around his cigarette and took a hurried drag, needing the nicotine rush to get him through the rest of the day. The prison of Finchley Hall seemed ever so dreary now that summer had gone and the cold was starting to set in.

He took one long look at the gloomy house, and his brow furrowed. He could do this. With just the promise that, once he did, he could leave and take Sebastian with him.

Smiling at the thought, he swooped ahead and hurried up the winding steps and into Finchley Hall. When he entered the hallway, Hugo paused on the mat.

The hearty boom of merry laughter came from down the hall. It blended in with clinking of cutlery and glasses, where the Harringtons and company took luncheon. Behind him, Sebastian arrived and dropped their cases onto the hallway floor. He too caught the chortling laughter and paused.

"Lord Montgomery..." he observed.

"Indeed. Sebastian, do take the afternoon off. You must be exhausted. I don't need you until, say, five."

"Very kind of you, sir," he said and proceeded to carry the luggage away.

Hugo hesitated, unsure what was deemed proper etiquette by the Harringtons. He was hungry, starving even, but was appearing midway through luncheon appropriate? Definitely not.

Hugo grumbled, and his stomach growled. He puffed harder at his cigarette, stuffed a hand into his pocket, and retreated to the yellow drawing room instead.

An hour later, the burly beast of a man bobbed his way into the lounge. Uncle Henry followed behind him.

"Oho! Talk of the devil and he shall appear," Montgomery roared. "My boy! How are you? Good trip? You look positively done for."

Hugo grinned and got quickly to his feet. "Lord Montgomery, pleasure to see you again."

Montgomery gripped his hand and shook it firmly. He pulled Hugo in for a frightfully enthusiastic hug and slapped him on the back.

"Don't mind if I talk to your uncle in private, eh? You and I must catch up this evening, though. Wouldn't leave an old man in his own company, would you?"

Hugo frowned, confused.

"I have to take a trip to Manchester at dawn, Hugo," Henry began. "I thought you'd like to entertain Jacob this evening."

Hugo opened his mouth to confirm, but Montgomery cut him off.

"Two nights of me and Henry's running away." He chortled.

Hugo forced a smile. This would not sit well with Sebastian. "Certainly. I'll see you soon. I'm going to take luncheon now. Nice to see you, Uncle Henry."

Henry nodded. Hugo made his way out of the lounge to eat...and mentally prepare himself for an evening of Jacob Montgomery.

HUGO LEANED AGAINST the open conservatory door with another cigarette stuck between his teeth. Here, in this quiet corner of Finchley Hall, disturbance was rare. Hugo hoped that Montgomery had tired himself out enough that he would cease his search for him and retire to bed. That, however, seemed most unlikely.

Cool air swept in from the open door and made him shiver pleasantly. Hugo sucked at the edge of his cigarette, turned his face toward the sky, and blew the smoke. Sebastian often teased him for not inhaling.

After such a long trip home, his body was riddled with exhaustion. It was easy to lean here against the frame of the door and think of nothing but of how pretty sky looked on a somehow—after all that rain earlier—cloudless night. The stars reminded him of Sebastian now.

"Ahhhh. Here you are."

Hugo's jaw tightened. He leaned away from the doorframe and turned his head to look back at the man filling the hallway outside of the conservatory. He lingered there for a moment, unsteady, before stepping into the room. He cradled a cup of tea in his hands.

"I thought you wouldn't want to take alcohol tonight. You look shattered, my boy," Montgomery said, setting the cup onto the coffee table.

"Quite right, Lord Montgomery." He managed a smile.

"Your valet sent this down," he said, gesturing toward the cup.

"Goodness, he should have brought it down himself."

Jacob shrugged. "Could I harass you for a cigarette?"

"Certainly." He plucked a new one from his tin, handed it over, and swept to stand by the coffee table and pick up the tea.

His gaze followed Montgomery as he lit the cigarette and made himself comfy on the sofa, crossing his legs and slouching back against the cushions. It was difficult to tell how drunk Montgomery was, though he really did seem like he needed that seat.

Hugo sipped at the tea, his nose wrinkled a bit, a little too herby for his liking. Seb should know by now that he only cared for black teas, but Jacob had made the effort of carrying it down for him, so out of politeness, he continued to sip.

"Do tell me all about your trip, Hugo."

Hugo smiled over the rim of his cup, raising a brow. "I feel like you're expecting I have some kind of scandalous tale to tell."

"Of course. You know how much I enjoy those types of stories. We both know I'm no angel."

"I'm afraid you'll be disappointed."

Montgomery suddenly straightened up and scoffed. "Oh come. Three days away with only a valet for company. You must have found some way to really amuse yourself."

Hugo's smile widened.

"I knew it! I knew it," Jacob said. "Come on. Let old Monty hear a little something taboo."

"Fine." Hugo sighed. He walked over to the sofa and perched himself on the edge beside the man. He finished up the tea and placed the cup down.

It took little effort to invent a story about a prostitute with red hair and big breasts. Hugo wasn't so sure why he was lying in such detail instead of simply denying he did anything. Perhaps it would ease Jacob off him a little. He didn't want to be prompted too hard and then spill what really happened in London.

By the time he was done and Montgomery had probed him for every explicit detail, Hugo's eyes were leaden with exhaustion. His limbs ached numbly; his senses were blurred and slow. Everything looked as if he'd just woken from slumber, slow and muffled and unclear.

Montgomery dropped a hand onto his thigh. Hugo drew his eyebrows together. He stared at the resting hand and opened his mouth to say something, but the words came out in slurred mumbles of nothing. Empty, hollow sounds. What was wrong with him?

Montgomery squeezed at his thigh with his great big hand, then slid it further up his leg. Hugo sucked in his stomach, and his breath hitched into a panicked rasp.

His head lolloped back. His eyes closed. The world rocked beneath him, and it made Hugo groan in fear. Something was up. This was wrong. This was bad.

"Don't you like it, Hugo?" Montgomery's voice, like a serpent, hissed into his ear. "I'm not a fool. I know you have perverted thoughts about men." A low, ragged growl. "I've seen the way you look at your valet." Montgomery's teeth were at his neck.

Hugo shrieked. His lids flew open. He threw himself forward and dragged himself off the sofa.

Standing, his legs wobbled unsteadily beneath him. He staggered forward, nudging his teacup off the edge of the coffee table, where it shattered across the floorboards.

"Se-Seb." Hugo's voice cracked. The words were merely a puff of air. His head reeled, his heart surged, stomach churned. Montgomery seized him by his shoulders, and he was thrown into the wall.

Hugo's back thudded against the surface, and he groaned, the air thrust from his lungs. His head drooped forward. "N-no..." he whispered, and something heavy fell over his chest and pinned him still against the wall. Hugo hadn't realised how much he had been squirming.

"Hugo?" A familiar voice radiated from somewhere behind the looming beast of Montgomery.

"Seb," Hugo groaned, whimpering in desperation. He reached out towards the sound. There was a dull thud and Montgomery groaned in pain.

Sebastian grabbed the monster by his shirt and pulled him away from the trembling mess of Hugo.

"Sebastian," he groaned again. Watching through glazed-over eyes as Sebastian punched Montgomery square in the face again and again until blood streamed from the man's nose.

Fuelled by blind rage, Sebastian threw punches until both he and Montgomery were soaked in red.

Somehow, Sebastian managed to wrestle the beast to the floor. He was on top of him then, and Montgomery screamed out gurgled cries of pain between his rasping breaths.

"S...s-stop." Hugo reached out, grasping at air. He didn't want him to get hurt, didn't want Montgomery to retaliate, but it was too late. Sebastian's screams of pain echoed in the room.

Hugo's legs bucked beneath him. His knees met the floor. Thompson appeared in the doorway.

Sebastian was seized and torn away from Montgomery, still yelling. "He was touching Hugo! He was hurting Hugo! He's an animal, Thompson! I'm going *to kill him!*"

Thompson's voice was a mess of noise. Hugo toppled forwards until he hit the floor hard. There was a scream of his name, and there was darkness.

Sixteen: The Letter

HIS HEAD WAS on fire. A searing pain flashed across his skull and radiated behind his eyes. The world swayed about him.

Beneath the sheets, his limbs trembled, his teeth chattered. The effect of the drugs had been hard for him to get over. Two days in bed, served by George, a gentle-spoken footman with a polite smile. No Sebastian. He hadn't heard from Sebastian. Perhaps he too was recovering. He hadn't looked so good after Montgomery was done with him.

The vomiting had been relentless. He sat, cradling a sick bowl in the crook of his arm. He felt clammy and pale with the taste of acid sharp on his tongue. Aunt Ethel had swept in and out often to see how he was doing. He'd never seen her look so motherly. With pretty eyes that were his mother's and a sweet voice that was almost hers too. She spoke to him softly, gently, without once questioning what had happened in the conservatory with Montgomery.

Sometimes she wiped over his forehead with a cold cloth and carded her fingers back through his hair. She urged him to sip at his water and chastised him to sleep. Hugo slept as much as he could. He craved the escape from it all.

However, the times spent not sleeping were filled with thinking about Sebastian. How was he? George would only tell him he was fine, not injured too badly. So why wouldn't he come upstairs to see him?

Hugo couldn't sit around and wait to see how his Sebastian was coping. Now he could sit up for longer than thirty minutes at a time, Hugo refused to simply sit and wonder.

He pulled the covers off and swung his legs over the bed. He stood up, and it took a few moments for the room to stop swaying enough for him to make a move. Slowly, he ambled towards the door, picking up his plum dressing gown and slipping into it as he went.

It was early. The birds cooed from their perches and the sun was creeping out of her place, hidden beneath her blankets of the horizon. The servants would be awake. The Harringtons would not.

He crept downstairs, pausing halfway down the steps. He was out of breath and his hands shook. Whatever Montgomery had put into his tea, it had really taken its toll on him. Lifting his hand to his head, he pressed the heel of his palm to his eyes and whined. This was hard.

"Is everything alright, sir?"

Hugo looked down. Thompson appeared at the foot of the stairs. He was angling his head to look up at Hugo and furrowed his brow. Everybody had been soft tones and sweet sympathetic smiles since it happened.

Hugo dropped his hand and shrugged. "I feel rather dizzy actually, Thompson. My darn ears keep ringing."

"Come, allow me to help you back to bed."

Hugo shook his head. "No, no. I came down because I wanted to find Seb. I knew ringing for him would only bring James."

"It's George, sir."

"George."

Thompson sighed. "We ought to talk." He stepped forward to head up the stairs.

"Please, can we talk downstairs? I can't face climbing all the way back up right now."

"Very well, sir." Thompson offered his arm.

With the butler's help, Hugo took the last few steps down into the servants' quarters. Through the glass doors, he saw every servant's head turn away from their breakfast to watch curiously as Hugo crossed by. He did wonder what sort of gossip happened downstairs. Perhaps quite a lot since the incident.

For a moment, he paused and careened his head to see if he could get a glimpse of Sebastian. He was not there.

"Is he so ill?" Hugo sighed. Thompson urged him to take a seat in his private quarters. He did.

Thompson looked down at Hugo, his face a hard, severe line. "Sebastian has been dismissed."

"*What?*" cried Hugo, getting up at once. "What do you mean dismissed? He can't be dismissed!"

"I am sorry, sir. Lord Harrington did not think it appropriate to keep him around after what happened to Lord Montgomery."

"He saved me from Montgomery!"

"He did, sir, but he also broke Lord Montgomery's nose, wrist, and as I hear, a couple of ribs too. That is not appropriate behaviour for a valet, under any circumstances. All the same, Lord Montgomery made some very severe threats about what would happen if we kept Sebastian around. Sebastian offered to go...although I will say, he was provided with a glowing reference.. However, word gets around and I am afraid Montgomery's version of the story is very different. Rumours have already begun to spread."

"For goodness sake! Where did he go?"

"I have received no forwarding address, sir."

"Christ!"

Thompson frowned. Hugo glowered.

"You should not have allowed this to happen, Thompson. As far as I'm concerned, Sebastian is a hero."

"I'm afraid, sir, I did try. However, Sebastian had none of it. Lord Montgomery said some dreadful things about you, and if Sebastian wasn't gone, your name was going to be dragged through the mud. He has some good friends in the press."

Hugo kicked hard at the chair. "Bushwa," he snarled and all of a sudden burst into a fit of furious tears.

Thompson hesitated unsure of what to do to console a crying man. He reached out his hand and it lingered in the air for a moment, before he gently patted at Hugo's shoulder. "I did not realise you were so attached to Sebastian, sir."

Hugo howled and covered his face with his hands.

"I must tell you, without a doubt, you will not see Montgomery again. Lord Henry threatened him with the police. So, there is something of a silver lining. Sir, allow me to make you a cup of tea and fetch you a blanket."

Thompson left the room.

Hugo whimpered with sorrow, with complete and utter despair. His shoulders shook with it, his stomach twisted. Complete anguish swept over him until his body seized up and his sobs dissolved into rasping, shuddering breaths. Sebastian was gone. After those glorious three days together, after everything Sebastian had come to mean to Hugo, he was gone.

HUGO SAT PERCHED beneath a crooked tree with a sketch pad resting in his lap. It was a beautiful day. The sun was glorious in the sky, warming up the green hills of the countryside. April so far had been his favourite month of English weather. Mild, wet, with violet, fuchsia, and yellow flowers scattered over the hilltops.

It was a time for jumpers, park benches, and an abundance of smiling Brits who had all at once remembered they were alive.

It had only been a couple of months since Hugo had begun to leave the confines of Finchley Hall again. The loss of Sebastian had turned him into a hermit. He'd shut the light from his bedroom windows, kept his head in his books, and busied himself with sketches.

Sometimes, his friends came over. Aunt Ethel had forced two boys upon him—Matthew and Fred. They were soft spoken, all smiles, polite with a good sense of humour. Cambridge graduates.

They weren't the usual type of people that Hugo spent his time with, but the loneliness was getting to him, and Hugo was glad for the company. Even if that meant playing chess in the garden or simply strolling through the hilltops. There was no more late-night partying nor even the urge for it, and Aunt Ethel and Uncle Henry seemed very pleased with his "progress."

These days, Aunt Ethel smiled sadly at him. Cousin Arabella had stopped her gentle taunting. Uncle Henry was softer.

When he'd left Finchley Hall alone for the first time since the "incident," they'd waved him off enthusiastically, pleased smiles on their faces. Now he'd gotten into a routine, leaving every day at noon for a stroll up the hill and to sit by the stream. He'd go with a basket prepared by Mrs. Greene and his sketch pad.

Today was his birthday, and so when he'd shrugged into his coat at twelve to leave, Aunt Ethel seemed somewhat stunned.

"But...Hugo...it's your birthday. Don't you want to have birthday luncheon with us? Frederick and Matthew will be here shortly."

"Sure, Aunt Ethel, I'll only be an hour."

"Okay, well, please don't be any longer. We'd like to spend family time with you. Here, take your birthday cards and maybe read them whilst you're out." She tucked the envelope into the basket lid. She'd kissed him gently on the cheek, and Hugo left.

Hugo sat, slouched against the tree, suddenly remembering of his cards. He flipped the sketch pad closed and pulled them from his basket.

Cards from cousins he scarcely saw, the Harringtons, the few friends he had made during his time here. The last one however was a surprise. Tucked in the corner was an American postage stamp. He ran his thumb across it and flipped the card over. From home. The first piece of mail from home. He ran his finger beneath the seal and opened the envelope up, then slipped out the card and opened it up.

Dearest Hugo,

We have missed you dearly. Your Aunt and Uncle have been keeping us up to date on your time in England and how you have learned to become something of a gentleman. It's been wonderful to know how you have conducted yourself, how you have adapted to English lifestyle and customs and readily involved yourself in the running your Uncle Henry's business.

It sounded like a damn business letter. Hugo scowled.

Most fascinating of all, we've heard how this nonsense partying and reckless behavior has stopped...after a rather bumpy start. Your father and I wanted to tell you how proud we are and how pleased we are that you have blossomed into a true gentleman. For your 21st birthday, we wish you all the best.
Our gift to you, is to inform you that your trust fund has been granted, and your full inheritance will be given. It's time for you to move on after all your efforts and we have provided you with the means to do so. We'd be delighted if you returned home to America but understand if you have fallen too in love with England. Happy birthday, dear Hugo.

Love Mom and Pops

Hugo tipped back his head and threw out a delighted laugh. Of course he'd be returning to America.

Seventeen: The New World

MUCH TO THOMPSON'S dismay, Hugo had insisted upon clearing away his room himself. There was something sacred about it. It was a ritual. He found therapy in folding away his belongings piece by piece, watching his sacred space return to the ghostly shell it had been when he moved here. All personal touches were taken down and dismantled. It was the closure he had needed.

Hugo opened his wardrobe and looked across the last pieces of clothing: his beloved mustard coat, the burgundy velvet dinner jacket he'd never worn, and a navy woollen scarf, still folded up on the shelf. He paused and reached up to grab it. Taking the material, he ran it through his fingers and sighed. He pressed it to his face and smiled against it. It smelled like Seb. God, he missed him.

Hugo wound the scarf around his neck and exhaled deeply. At least he was going home. Back to the glamour of the city, back to jazz and illicit clubs, back to where he belonged...so he'd thought. But perhaps he'd outgrown that too.

There was a knock at his door.

"Come in." Hugo closed his wardrobe doors. He turned to see Thompson hovering in his doorway, those soft eyes of his drifted about his bare walls with a look of sadness falling over his expression.

"Ah, sir, you will be terribly missed."

Hugo laughed. "Oh come off it. You must all breathe a sigh of relief when you no longer need to worry about what kind of trouble I'm getting myself into."

"On the contrary, sir, you added so much life to Finchley Hall. We will be very sorry to see you go."

Hugo smiled sadly. "Funnily enough, I'm not entirely delighted to be going back to America. I've grown sort of fond of this place." Sort of...

"It does have a certain charm."

"It really does," Hugo hummed. He could say he'd be back to visit one day, but that didn't feel genuine. He looked down at Thompson's hands. He was clutching a bundle of letters. "Are those for me?"

Thompson cleared his throat. "Oh, sorry, they are, sir. Your last bit of mail before you leave."

"Thanks, Thompson." He took them and stuffed them straight into his inner pocket.

"But most of all, I was looking for an excuse to see if I could steal a hug before you made your way back."

Hugo laughed and opened his arms. "I thought you'd never ask, dear Thompson. Thank you for everything you have done." Thompson wrapped strong arms around his frame and patted him on the back. It was time for him to make a move.

"I'll send up the footmen to bring down your luggage whilst you say goodbye to your family."

Hugo stepped back from Thompson's embrace and fixed him a genuine warm smile. "Goodbye, Thompson."

"Goodbye, sir."

Saying goodbye to the Harringtons was easy. Like on the day he arrived, the entire household lined up side by side in the garden, looking a little friendlier than the first time.

Thompson beamed, and most incredibly of all, so did Uncle Henry. The man shook his hand firmly whilst they stood on the balcony overlooking the grounds. He slapped him on the shoulder and yanked him into a hug.

Aunt Ethel kissed him on both of his cheeks before scooting back to dab beneath her eyes with a lace handkerchief. Arabella sobbed, and her bottom lip stuck out and wobbled. She threw her arms around Hugo and he patted her on the head reluctantly. They'd barely exchanged a word. What a ridiculously dramatic response to his goodbyes.

Hugo ruffled up her hair, and she squeaked, pulling back immediately.

She threw him a little glare and laughed. "Goodbye, cousin. Do come back and visit."

Hugo lifted his hand and waved. "Goodbye, darling Arabella. I will, if you at least write."

Hugo stepped down the marble steps of Finchley Hall for the final time and disappeared into the waiting car, desperate to escape the clutches of the Harringtons and drive away as a free independent man.

Charles closed the door and scurried into the front, and at last, they roared towards the open gates. He faced forward and didn't look back again.

He shrugged out of his jacket and let it fall onto the seat behind him. Sticking out of his inner pocket was a white corner.

"How long a drive is it, Charles? I forgot." Or rather, he'd fallen asleep on the way here.

"About three hours, sir."

Hugo huffed and pulled out the bundle of letters. Looking down at the beautiful cursive on the top one, his heart skipped a beat. Hugo froze. It looked an awful lot like Sebastian's handwriting. He could practically hear the sarcastic groan of his name in Sebastian's voice as he read it.

A brief smile flickered over his mouth, and he flipped the envelope over and tore it open. Unfolding the letter, his heart warbled with excitement, his eyes fluttered to the end of the letter, and sure enough, there was his name signed at the bottom.

"Sebastian," he cooed.

Hugo,

Sorry I have not written to you before now. I didn't have a returning address and I've had to keep a low profile. I find that people like Montgomery, with too much power, have a lot of influence on people's decision-making and it seemed that word had gotten around about what I did to him.

Finding work has been an incredibly gruelling task. Valet work seems to be available less and less these days. Anyway, this isn't about me. I wanted to wish you a belated happy birthday. I assume you'll be returning to America shortly, so I just wanted to say what a delight it has been working for you. Please take care of yourself, Hugo, and know that you will always be in my thoughts. This chapter has come to an end, but I know you will find great happiness in your next story.

All the best.

Always yours,
Sebastian

Hugo swallowed. Tears brimmed in his eyes. He pressed the letter against his chest. Was that it? Was this all he had to say after everything?

He looked back at the letter, at the address on the top right, and glared. "Charles! Charles! We have to make a detour!" He looked up and met the man's eyes in the rear-view mirror.

Charles let out a long-suffering groan.

THE TOWN FROM the letter was a very simple place, quiet with cobbled streets and endless lines of grey stone houses with brightly painted front doors. It was made up of narrow alleyways and a village hall, with a single church and little shops.

Hugo peered out of the window and his brow furrowed as they drove down the petite streets, turning every head they passed. "These houses are like matchstick boxes; how do people live in them?"

"It's how most people live, sir," Charles answered dryly.

"Why are they all looking at us?"

"We're in a car..."

"Oh." Hugo ruffled his hair and leaned further forward, straining to see the door numbers. Eleven, thirteen... "Charles, we're almost there. Twenty-one!"

The car pulled up against the sidewalk, and Charles switched off the engine. Hugo sat for a moment and pressed his lips together. His hand drifted towards the handle, but then he paused and dropped it again. He huffed in frustration.

"What if he's angry that I came to see him?"

"Then he's angry and we just continue on, but I think he'd be flattered more than anything. Perhaps a little sad. This isn't the life I imagined he'd have now."

"What do you mean?"

"Well, this is a different world to the comfort of Finchley Hall."

"And this is how he was thanked for saving me." Hugo wrinkled his brow and nodded sharply. "I have a plan." He flung open the car door and stepped out onto the sidewalk.

For a moment, he hesitated outside of the maroon door. Before he could even knock, the door was pulled open and a tall skinny man with copper hair sticking out at all angles threw him an alarmed look.

"Who are you?"

Hugo stared at the man and took an equally alarmed step back. "Oh. No. I'm looking for Sebastian. Does he live here?"

"You're Finch's friend?" The man snorted, his gaze roaming over Hugo. He muttered something else, but the accent was too thick and Hugo couldn't quite understand what he was saying. The man finished with a booming laugh, and Hugo felt the need to laugh quietly too, as if he'd understood a joke.

"Ah, he'll be home in about half an hour. If you give us a pack of cigarettes, might let you wait inside with a cuppa."

"With a cuppa what?"

He didn't explain, only grabbed Hugo by the arm and tugged him into the hall.

The house was a box. Separated into a few smaller rooms. The kitchen was cosy. With a stone stove and a little table in the corner crammed with a fruit bowl in the centre and a thick blanket thrown over each chair. Most of all, it was cold and a breeze came in through the crack in the back door.

"Cosy, eh?" the man said as he rooted around in his cupboards for two cups. Hugo sat down in a rigid chair and didn't answer the question, but the man continued on.

"They're quite good to us factory workers. Got this village set up for us all. Rent is low, there's no crime, it's clean. You an inspector or something? You're obviously not a friend of Sebastian's really."

"Why do you live with him?" Hugo said very suddenly, unable to help himself. The man seemed quite a lot older than Sebastian and certainly not Sebastian's taste. He was all callused hands, with a face like tan leather and whispers of grey in his hair.

The man paused and turned his head to shoot Hugo a surprised look. "Well, it's cheaper. I'm a widower; Sebastian is young and single. He was homeless when we met at the pub. I sorted him out with a job, and he pays me some rent, helps me out quite a lot really."

"Homeless?" Hugo repeated, his jaw tightening. He let out of length of curses and gripped at the corner of the table. Suddenly, his fist met the surface of the wood. "For goodness sake!"

"Oi! Watch it!"

"Sorry," Hugo groaned, his face burning. He reached into his pocket, pulled out his carton of cigarettes, took one out for himself, and threw the remainder of the packet onto the table for the man. Biting at the tip, he struck his lighter and sparked up.

The man turned his back again and then brought over a pot of tea. He set it in the middle of the table and placed a tin of biscuits beside it. He muttered something under his breath and returned to fetch mugs, milk, and the sugar bowl. Hugo took the handle and poured them both a mug full of tea, then added a lump of sugar and a splash of milk.

"Really, though, how'd you know Finch?"

Hugo took a sip of his tea and set the cup back down. "He was my valet. My family dismissed him because he protected me from assault by hitting an aristocrat square in the face."

The man snorted. "No way!"

Hugo nodded. "I've come to take him back, if he'll have it. I'll pay you his rent for the next four months so you don't need to worry about any losses until you can find a new lodger."

The man leaned back and raised a brow. "You fancy people..." And once again, he went into a ramble of unintelligible accented muttering.

Hugo sipped at his tea and puffed at his cigarette desperately. He glanced up at the clock, and there came the metallic click of the door and a voice that sent a heat of giddy warmth to Hugo's chest.

"Peter, there's a fancy car parked at the bottom of the street. Whose is it?" he called from the hallway.

Hugo couldn't wait. He dropped his cup, stubbed out his cigarette, and got to his feet. He swept into the hallway and froze at the sight of him. His face was dirty, his hair stuck out beneath a flat cap, and he was dressed in grey. He didn't look like Sebastian. He looked like a factory worker.

"Seb," he whispered.

"*Hugo?*" Sebastian said, removing his cap. His hair beneath was wild and unruly. He hooked up his cap and shrugged out of his coat, revealing his willowy frame. "Whoa. Hugo. What are you doing here?"

Hugo only smiled, and in an instant, he was crying. Loud and helpless, until his shoulders trembled with it. "I'm so sorry this has happened to you, Sebastian," he sobbed, tears spilling across his cheeks.

Sebastian crossed over to him and rested a hand on his shoulder. "Don't cry, Hugo. I'm okay now, I'm fine." He kissed his forehead quickly.

Hugo threw his arms around him and squeezed him tightly. "I wish I knew. I'd have helped you. Why didn't you tell me you were going?"

"There was no time. The police were going to be called. It was a mess. I was being shooed out by Thompson who was worried about me. Montgomery made some threats, and I didn't want you to get roped into this. So I left," Sebastian cooed, his voice sweet and light. He rubbed Hugo's arm and patted him on the shoulder. "But don't worry about me. I'm working now."

"In a factory." Hugo sniffled.

"It pays my way."

Hugo took a step back and looked up at Sebastian, frowning. "I'm going to America."

Sebastian looked a little startled but forced a big smile across his face. "Yeah? I thought you might. We should catch up before you go. When's the day?"

"Right now," he answered, rubbing at his eyes.

"Now?" Sebastian tried to hide the disappointment in his voice but didn't manage so well. "Right now?"

Hugo nodded.

Sebastian cursed.

Hugo tipped back his head and looked up at the man, desperation darkened his eyes. He sought purchase in the folds of his dirty shirt. "Come with me."

"To America?"

Hugo nodded.

"I don't...know." Sebastian's face fell, confusion written across his features. He looked back at Hugo, nipping at his lip with his teeth. "I can't just up and leave on a whim."

"Yes, you can!" Hugo laughed and tugged at Sebastian's shirt. "I'll get you a ticket. If there's no room on this departure, we'll wait until there is. Come, Sebastian. Come with me."

"Your parents will approve?"

"I'm twenty-one. I have my own money now. I'm going to get my own place. You can run my house. You can be my butler, my valet, my man. Please, Sebastian. I need you," Hugo pleaded, his eyes growing wide. He stared up into those beautiful brown eyes and felt himself begin to melt beneath that soft, loving gaze. "Please," he whispered again. "What have you got to lose?"

"Nothing," Sebastian said simply. "I'll come. Of course I'll come." Sebastian laughed full-heartedly, suddenly alight with excitement at the prospect. He pulled Hugo closer, only slightly wary of the man in the next room and planted a kiss on the top of his head. Perhaps everything was going to be okay.

"YOU MISSED A spot, Hugo," Sebastian cooed. He clutched a cup of coffee in his hand and slouched back in the leather armchair by the great fireplace. Hugo's new home was cosy—rustic with fireplaces and thick rugs and obscure paintings on the walls.

He took pride in the fine crystal and wood furnishings that Sebastian cursed for taking forever to polish, but it wasn't necessarily always Sebastian doing the cleaning.

Today, Sebastian had him in the lounge, Hugo's favourite room, for the window faced out into the gardens at the back of the house. Natural light spilled into the room, and with Hugo leaning across the oak coffee table in nothing but an apron, he was sure Sebastian got a lovely view of his naked ass.

Hard as he was, his cock bobbed gently with the motion of his hand working circles along the tabletop, sweeping back and forth.

"What've I told you about how to position yourself when you clean my table like this?" Sebastian huffed. He placed the cup down on the table.

Hugo cursed but spread his legs wider apart, and now, Sebastian got a beautiful view of his pink asshole.

"Good. Much better."

"I knew the power would get to your head," Hugo grunted, his cheeks on fire.

"And to your cock, apparently. Funny how things change, hmm?"

"Enjoy it whilst it lasts, *sir*."

"Oh I will, Hugo, I will."

About the Author

SJ hails from a quaint, modest town in the north of England. However, for the past three years, she has been swept up in the whirlwind of London life, where people don't make eye contact. Admittedly, she only moved here for the theatre.

A self-confessed geek; lover of the history, travelling and musicals. SJ loves to spend her weekends in museums, wandering around antique bookshops, or finding new, quirky places to explore. She feels blessed to be from a multi-cultural background, with an Irish mother and an African father.

Soppy as she is, you can be sure to find light-hearted, fluffy books from this author, with just a light sprinkle of feels.

Email: sjfoxxauthor@gmail.com

Twitter: www.twitter.com/SjFoxx

Website: www.sjfoxx.wordpress.com/

Also Available from NineStar Press

Connect with NineStar Press

www.ninestarpress.com

www.facebook.com/ninestarpress

www.facebook.com/groups/NineStarNiche

www.twitter.com/ninestarpress

www.tumblr.com/blog/ninestarpress